Praise for The Wenamak Web:

"Howalt writes in the vein of Becky Chambers, making this a hell of a good time. A lot is packed into this novella. I'm coming out of it broken and healed."

— Nathaniel Luscombe, author of *Moon Soul*

"A beautiful dance of characters with slices of life in space that keeps the pages turning and the universe feeling alive."

— Aden Ng, author of *The Chronicles of Tearha*

"*The Wenamak Web* is a well-structured novel that is balanced and deft, and (...) examines the social and political implications of inter-species relationships. Fans of science fiction with elaborately developed characters, a phenomenal conflict, and a stunningly imagined world will find this tale absorbing."

— Cristina Prescott, *The Book Commentary*

"In the third installment of the Colibri series, *The Wenamak Web*, Marie Howalt pulls the reader into a frantic dive into the underground of Wenamak, a wonderful planet where it's impossible to lie and yet nurses a very dark side. Clever, entertaining and full of action, *The Wenamak Web* is a wonder mix of science-fiction and old school hard-boiled crime stories. Totally recommended."

— Seb Doubinsky, author of *The Sum of All Things*, *The Horror*, and *Paperclip*

"Richard, Eddie, and Alannah are back again for another adventure. Howalt has created a casually inclusive world where disability is accommodated without fuss, difference is accepted, and second chances are granted. A light, easy read!"

— Si Clarke, author of *The Left Hand of Dog*

"*Colibri Investigations* is the sci-fi series you didn't know you needed. It's a fun, and at times thought provoking ride with characters you can't help but fall in love with from page 1. Once you start reading, you won't be able to stop. If you're tired of samey sci-fi, *Colibri Investigations* is the breath of fresh air you've been waiting for, with a vibrant, carefully thought out world. If you like Douglas Adams or John Scalzi, you'll love this."

— Kathy Joy, author of *Last One to the Bridge*

"Funny and serious, sweet and rough - *The Wenamak Web* is a wonderful blend, with characters you get to love and sometimes want to kick for being stupid."

—Jane Mondrup, author of *Zeitgeist* and *Zoi*

Other Works by Marie Howalt

***Colibri* Investigations**
The Stellar Snow Job (2022)
Assassins & Olympians (2023)

The Moonless Trilogy
We Lost the Sky (2019)
Seeking Shelter (2020)
Heart of the Storm (2021)

A Moonless Novelette
Training Wheels (2021)

COLIBRI INVESTIGATIONS

THE WENAMAK WEB

MARIE HOWALT

Denver, Colorado

Published in the United States by:
Spaceboy Books LLC
1627 Vine Street
Denver, CO 80206
www.readspaceboy.com

Cover art features CC0 art by GarryKillian via Pixabay

ISBN: 978-1-951393-41-0
First printed September 2024

For everyone who needs a space to breathe

The lavpolk virus is an example of viral strains that were assumed harmless when first brought to the attention of the Human Health Concern Agency. As it only afflicted zetois among all the native species on Alhm, it was believed that it would not attack any alien lifeforms either. To zetois, the lavpolk virus is a minor inconvenience akin to any upper respiratory infection (aka URI or a common cold) that humans can contract. It results in a rise in body temperature and a sensation of sluggishness for a few days, and while unpleasant, nearly all zetois (with the exception of those with comorbid diseases who require medical assistance to rid their bodies of viral infections) recover fully on their own. In fact, it is the testament to the harmlessness of the illness that no great efforts have been made by the zetois themselves to eradicate it.

Recently, however, the HHCA issued a warning regarding the very same virus strain. During deployment on Ikhlm in connection with the establishment of a Terran embassy in this relatively new zetoi settlement, a Terran Defense Force officer came into contact with a zetoi going to work despite having symptoms of the lavpolk virus. The officer contracted said virus and developed symptoms within 24 standard Earth hours.

Although the two species can thrive under the same atmospheric conditions and on similar diets, human physiology is very different from that of a zetoi. To name the most obvious dissimilarity, humans are mammals whereas zetois are avians.

Interestingly, the human officer's symptoms were much more severe than the zetoi's right from the onset. The body temperature of the officer rose alarmingly, and he was quickly hospitalized. He also suffered from joint and muscle pain as well as what was believed to be cognitive difficulties at first.

Scans of the officer's brain at the time (fig. 4) show the virus attacking certain parts in his brain, particularly Wernicke's area. It soon became apparent that connections vital to the human brain's ability to process speech were severed by the virus. The patient gradually recovered from the fever and pain over the course of four weeks. The speech processing disorder, however, did not change significantly, as you can see from the subsequent scans (fig. 5-7). Nanotechnology and surgery also did not improve the officer's ability to discern speech as the lavpolk virus caused the relevant connections to actively reject repairs in a manner much like certain autoimmune diseases. It appears, in other words, that the auditory verbal agnosia experienced by the officer is permanent.

Appendix C is a compilation of interviews in which the officer describes his symptoms during and after the illness.

— Excerpt from internal Human Health Concern Agency study

1

CATCHING UP

Wenamak was one of the first planets to be included in the wendek diaspora and as such, the species had lived there for several standard Earth centuries at this point. That was plenty of time to establish cities with every convenience and inconvenience a modern settlement by a category 3 species, be it human, wendek or something else entirely, was likely to boast. The primary city, Kwipadam, had a commercial district, educational institutions, living areas, and all the entertainment and recreation possibilities you would expect of the wendek. It also had neighborhoods where a high percentage of the population was mostly made up of other species.

The address private investigator Richard Hart was searching for was located in exactly one such area. It was not a polished, colorful part of the city. If pressed, Richard might even call it a slum. There was a run-down air here and half of the buildings looked like they ought to be torn down or thoroughly renovated. Most of the people he met were fellow humans. The occasional draever with mottled green or brown skin shouldered past him, though, taller and quite a lot broader than Richard himself although he was by no means small for a human. When Richard met a wendek on his way, they appeared to be in a hurry to get somewhere else.

Richard had left his pilot and cultural consultant on board his spaceship, the *Colibri*, which was docked at Wenamak's local space station. The message that brought him to Kwipadam had indicated that it was a business rather than a social call. Richard was armed as a precaution, but he did not expect to need weapons when visiting an acquaintance, so his dart gun holster was sitting out of sight inside his vaguely military-cut jacket.

Wendek usually wore their hair long and colorful and had practically no facial hair, but Richard wasn't going to change his short and increasingly salt-and-pepper hair or his fashionable stubble to blend in. And despite the wendek's preference for layered clothes and cinched waists, Richard had opted for a pair of comfortable pants with multiple pockets and a loose shirt which gave him a silhouette that would never be mistaken for a wendek's. Well, wendek usually had no objections against humans except their smell, and besides, Richard was meeting a fellow human today.

He raised his hand and touched his wristband. His patch was a sturdy, practical model with lots of fancy functions, but what Richard needed right now was just a map. The high-speed PlaNet connection made sure it was immediately updated with his current position upon arriving on the planet, and it had not dropped once since then. One left turn and Richard would reach the right location. His old acquaintance had not volunteered any details as to the reason for wanting to see him apart from hinting that it was about a favor or a job.

They had not been in touch for years, and what exactly he— No, Richard mentally scolded himself, Chrys used she now. What exactly she meant by that, he would find out soon enough. He made his way across the street and sideways between two parked groundwheelers. They were so close to each other that even their rotatable wheels would have difficulties getting them onto the street from that position.

The sign over the door said 'medical clinic' in four different languages. Standard, English, Draspaarg, and one of the wendek languages. Richard couldn't tell which, but a qualified guess was Synal since that was the prominent language on Wenamak.

The front door slid open as Richard approached. It emitted a low chime to alert the staff that someone had arrived.

The waiting room was everything you would expect. The walls were covered in screens and posters. One screen informed him that the doctor was currently busy and to please scan his patch at the self-service stand and then wait. Richard decided that message was for patients and not private investigators coming in to potentially pick up a case.

The bigger screen on the wall ran a loop of advertisements for various medications which felt both logical and a bit tasteless in a medical clinic, especially if the companies behind the drugs paid the doctor to recommend them. The posters were mostly informative. Something about a vaccination for a wendek flu that went around and another on free examinations for certain human conditions.

Richard sat down in one of the chairs in the small waiting room. The floor was scuffed in places, and the cushions on the chairs were worn, but everything looked and smelled clean and slightly antiseptic. Occasionally, the water dispenser gurgled in a strangely soothing way.

He was sifting through the informational dispatches that tended to appear on your patch when arriving on a new planet when a person came through a door in the back of the waiting room. It was another human, unsurprisingly. They walked past Richard and out of the front door without acknowledging him.

A moment later, another person appeared, wiping her hands. Her blond hair was gathered in a messy bun spilling strands over her face, and her lab coat screamed healthcare professional, which was exactly what she was.

"Richard Hart," she said, smiling. "Thank you for coming so soon."

"Hello, Chrys." Richard returned her smile and stood up, took a step toward her and then stopped.

"What?" she asked, crossing her arms over her chest.

"I was wondering if we hug, but you are..." He trailed off and made an indistinct gesture up and down her body.

"Really, Richard?" she huffed. "You only hug people who present as male?"

"No!" Richard protested. "Give me some credit! I meant you are wearing your work clothes and I've only had the rudimentary decontamination when I arrived in Kwipadam's spaceport."

"Oh. Right," Chrys replied, uncrossing her arms again. "Thank you for considering it, but I don't have any more scheduled patients today, and I can quickly decontaminate if something comes up. We can hug."

Richard smiled and folded his arms around her, giving her a quick squeeze.

She said something.

Richard stepped back so he could see her face. "Pardon?" he asked while a small voice in the back of his head added, "Here we go again." He hated this part. He hated having to explain, and although he had adjusted perfectly well, he always felt a tiny bit fake telling someone new how positively fine and dandy everything was.

"I said, I was surprised to learn you're back in the civilian ranks now. How come you quit? If you don't mind me asking."

"I was discharged for medical reasons," Richard told her. "So, do you want to talk here or go somewhere else?"

The doctor quickly sized him up with her gaze, looking for the medical reason in question, probably. "I am still on call for emergencies for another hour, so I'd prefer to stay here. Do you want a cup of black brew? It's not the best, but it does the job."

"I am pretty sure I have had worse," Richard said, which was entirely true. In a galaxy where every client, apart from one particular Terran Defense Force Colonel, offered him humanity's default beverage, he had come across everything from the cheapest black brew available to actual coffee. The latter only that once when he investigated a wealthy member of the governing body of one of the separationist settlements, though.

The doctor motioned for him to follow her into an adjacent room that, from the look of it, was a recreation or lunch room. It had a small table, two chairs, a cooler, and the ingredients for instant black brew. She retrieved two plass cups from a wall cupboard, emptied a sachet of instant black brew into each of them and poured hot water from a heated bottle. "Have a seat," she said, handing him one of the cups. "May I ask," she continued when they were both sitting, "about your medical condition? It's perfectly okay if it's none of my business. I'm just professionally curious."

"It's fine," Richard assured her. "I've come to terms with it." Which was true, on the whole. Sure, there were still days when he felt like punching a hole in the wall when people forgot and he had to remind them, but that wouldn't do. First of all because he lived on a spaceship, and secondly because there were better ways to deal with frustration. "Verbal auditory agnosia," he said. "I don't know if you are familiar with it?"

"Oh, that's good," Chrys said, then cleared her throat. "Sorry. What I mean is that I was worried you were terminally ill or had a terribly painful condition. I'm sure it's not that great when you are the one having to deal with it. It must take a lot of energy. So you lipread?"

Richard gave her a grateful nod. Her articulation hadn't changed notably at the revelation. Small mercies. "Yes. It's taken some getting used to, and some adjusting in everyday life," he admitted. Like keeping his spaceship silent and forfeiting music with vocals, which meant some of his favorite bands. "But enough about me. How are you?"

The doctor smiled. "Same old," she said. "Except now I'm living on Wenamak."

"Would it be tactless of me to say you look great?" Richard asked.

"No, not when you aren't here for medical assistance," Chrys replied with a smile. "Thank you. Anyway, I'm still mainly treating human patients, but there has been an influx of draevere lately too. Which, between you and me, is slightly daunting. I have a few courses under my belt, and I can treat common injuries, but anything beyond that... I tell them to see a qualified draever physician, but there's a certain clientele who prefers me over other doctors. And that brings me to the reason you're here. Or," she added, "not exactly, but it makes a good segue."

"By all means," Richard said, studying her over his cup. The black brew really was bland.

"There is a local gang here who illegally sells weapons to aliens, by which I mean primarily humans. The gang also runs an underground fighting ring where aliens are considered a hot, exotic commodity." She made a face at her own words, understandably disgusted by the terms. "Wealthy wendek like to see people of other species beat each other up and bet on them. Without breaking my doctor-patient confidentiality, I can tell you that I have treated some serious injuries those fighters have sustained."

Richard cocked his head. "And you want me to..?" he prompted.

"I am not the person who wants to hire you," she said.

"I see," Richard said, waiting for her to elaborate.

"A friend of mine wants to put an end to the gang's illegal activities, and he needs help with it. Specifically, he needs someone reliable and competent who isn't wendek. So he asked if I knew anyone, and, well, the rest is history," she concluded.

"I take your friend is wendek, then?" Richard asked.

"Yes, he is."

"I also take it that he holds a relevant position in wendek society and has the qualifications to do this?"

Chrys made a gesture that made no sense until Richard remembered that tapping the air with two fingers was the wendek equivalent of a nod. "He does. He's not a vigilante. This is his job."

Richard took another mouthful of the black brew, half regretting that he had accepted it. So this wendek friend was probably in the wendek peace corps or the security agency. "I don't usually get involved in the business of other species," he said. "It gets too complicated, legally speaking."

"My friend is taking the full responsibility," the doctor said, clearly intent on convincing him to take this job. "And in a way, this is human business. Humans are buying the weapons and getting beaten up in the fighting ring."

Richard could guess what the wendek wanted him to do. Pretend to want to buy illegal wares so there would be evidence. There must be other humans around who could do that, but he supposed Chrys had a point. Richard had the right credentials to pull it off smoothly. Except, of course, that the wendek arms dealers were literally able to smell that something was off, but the mysterious potential client must have a solution for that.

"Would you agree to meet with my friend and hear him out?" Chrys asked. "Please? As a favor for me?"

Richard sighed. "All right. I'm not saying I'll take the job. I need to discuss it with my associates, too. But let me have his contact info, and I'll get in touch with him."

Chrys visibly relaxed. "Thank you, Richard. I really appreciate it. I think it's easier if I tell him to contact you, though."

"No, it isn't," Richard said. He had suffered clandestine operations often enough to call undercover bullshit. "But I expect he asked you to facilitate the contact between us like that for some professionally secretive reason."

Chrys cleared her throat. "Well, yes," she admitted.

"Fine. When can I expect him to get in touch?"

"Later today. His name is Raithan." She smiled again. "Really, Richard, I appreciate this a lot."

"I haven't taken the job yet," Richard reminded her.

When humanity left the comfortable confines of our solar system and became part of the Union, we had a lot of homework to cram as fast as we possibly could. And it was not merely learning the rules of the peoples we shared the galaxy with.

We had to unlearn a lot of what our own limited scope and imagination had told us to expect. For instance, when it came to language, English or Arabic or Chinese or Latin or any other human tongue was of course incomprehensible to the species we met. We had to learn Standard which is, fittingly, the standard in communication between species in Category 3 (and 1, as it happens). All species have several native tongues of their own, however. Old Earth entertainment would usually present fictional extraterrestrial species as having only one language. But like humans don't speak "Human", wendek, for instance, do not speak "Wendek". They have a number of languages, Synal, Menal and Lai being but a few of them. Likewise, their home planet is not named after its dominating species. (In case you are not familiar with Menal and Synal, the "mak" you find in Ganmak as well as several settlement names translates roughly to "home".)

But language was not humanity's only challenge. We also had to face the vast differences between our own culture(s) and customs and those of other species.

Take wendek for example; they are the species most akin to us. They are mammals, bipedal, have the features we expect to see in a face and on a body. Most of us see wendek in general as attractive. Their skin may be various shades of grey instead of the brown/beige spectrum we find among humans, they may have a different ear shape, and they may be taller and more elongated than humans, and so on, but these are differences that are easily imaginable to us; something that is cemented by the fact that we have invented creatures very much like them in appearance long before we even knew they existed. (Please refer to the linked depictions of Tolkien's elves, *Star Trek*'s Vulcans, and *EverMist Isles*' dark elves as examples.)

Our civilizations have developed similarly (as is the case with several species in the Union), and we can directly relate to a lot of wendek popular culture. However, everything about wendek is not that simple to translate. In other words, there is not a human equivalent to everything wendek and vice versa. The most obvious physical feature to mention is, of course, the wendek sense of smell and use of pheromones, undetectable to humans, as means of communication.

Humans have opinions on smells, and yes, some smells do affect us without our consciously noticing. But that is nothing compared to wendek. What we pick up from facial expressions and body language, they understand by way of smells. Wendek will nearly always be able to tell the emotional state of someone else like this. They use smells in cooking, learning and recreational drugs and probably nearly anything else you can think of. If you have ever visited a wendek station or planetary settlement, you will know that you are banned from bringing certain odors because what you think of as a nice perfume may feel extremely intrusive or overwhelming to a wendek's sensitive nose. This is also why you will often meet wendek wearing facemasks or nose plugs when they are among other species.

As a human who has spent most of her childhood and teenage years on a wendek world, I can tell you that personal hygiene is of the utmost importance in order not to become an unwanted intrusion of smell.

— Alannah Jackson, *Why Wendek Are Not Space Elves*

2
NOT IN A MILLION LIGHT YEARS

Two glasses were sitting on the table in the *Colibri*'s galley between Eddie Macías and Alannah Jackson. The contents looked dull and inconspicuous, but they were anything but. Taarz was a popular draever drink of the non-alcoholic variety because Alannah had insisted it was too early in the local day cycle to be drinking, even if they had nothing to do before Richard returned to the *Colibri* from his mysterious meeting on Wenamak. What the drinks had going for them was taste. Taste that transformed into sinus clearing sharpness and felt like icepicks in your brain if you drank too fast or too much. But not in an entirely unpleasant way. Which meant icepicks probably wasn't the right word to use, anyway.

"All right," Alannah said, narrowing her eyes in concentration. "Not in a million light years have I gotten drunk on daazac."

Eddie blinked. Then picked up her glass and took a swig. And yelped as it went straight to her head in a burst of sparkles and pain. "You are doing this on purpose!" she wheezed. "Who the hell hasn't gotten drunk on daazac?"

Alannah's face lit up in the closest thing she ever got to a mischievous grin. Her dark eyes were full of laughter, and she theatrically brushed a stray lock of curly, pastel purple hair back over her shoulder. "Well, I haven't. I don't like the taste."

"It's never about the taste with draever drinks when you're human. Exhibit A," Eddie argued, gesturing to the glasses.

"Nevertheless," Alannah said, smugly.

Eddie chewed her lip, trying to find a statement that would turn the tables. It was a simple game with simple rules and a misleading name. One person made a statement about something they had never done, and everyone who had done it had to drink, or take off a clothing item, or whatever you agreed on before starting the game. If no one did, the person who made the statement would have to do it. It was invented with a bigger pool of people in mind, but Eddie was coming down from her last dose of hyper and needed something to keep her occupied. She had considered doing some minor maintenance on the *Colibri*, but nothing was broken, and she had been bored with the thought before she even began. Alannah, resourceful as always, had suggested this instead.

As it was, Alannah was wearing a pair of slippers along with a soft, comfortable outfit that made her look extremely cozy. Eddie herself didn't do that kind of fluffiness. She was all sharp edges, long limbs, and short, dark hair that was always a quick hyperjump away from falling in her eyes. Her idea of relaxed clothes wasn't very different from her idea of work clothes; a pair of tight ecoleather pants and whatever top happened to be clean and within reach. Anyway, their stakes for this game were not clothes but drinks.

"Okay. Not in a million light years have I watched a full episode of *The Garden of Singing Kelp!*" Eddie stated.

Alannah took a deep breath, raised her own glass and drank. She shuddered and made a small, whimpering noise that Eddie could not quite decide if she liked or hated. "I happen to like åayu entertainment!" she gasped.

"Please explain that to me," Eddie said. "Literally nothing happens in åayu shows!"

"That isn't true," Alannah said, clearing her throat and composing herself. "The writing is always great, the visuals and audio are stunning, and there are always characters you can relate to. And you can learn a lot."

"But nothing happens!" Eddie insisted. "*The Garden of Singing Kelp* is about some botanists or whatever swimming around and looking at, well, kelp."

"In one episode, they have to fight an invasive seagrass species. And there's a storyline where one of the botanists has an argument with xyr friend who prefers to stay mostly on land and it's really about the sacrifices you are willing to make for each other and how there has to be room for both parties in a friendship," Alannah said. "Yes, I have watched several episodes. I think it's a beautiful thing that entertainment doesn't have to involve crime and guns and fights."

Eddie clamped her mouth shut on an answer. She generally liked åayu. Honestly, who didn't? The little amphibians were a friendly bunch, explorers, scientists, honest merchants and respectful tourists. And they were the only species Eddie knew of who had never fucked up their homeworld with war or pollution. Maybe boring entertainment was the price they paid for that.

All right, so Eddie was an adrenaline junkie. Chasing a criminal, landing in a difficult environment, narrowly escaping trouble... Those were the things that got Eddie's blood pumping. And hyper. Maybe the prospect of thrills was the reason Eddie had so readily agreed to join Richard. Though in reality, not all of *Colibri* Investigations' missions were particularly exciting.

Their last job had basically been a background check on a person that a company wanted to hire for a high-profile position, and they had been able to dig up no dirt on the guy except a few bills paid too late a couple of years back. Sure, it was nice to get a simple case once in a while, one that didn't involve getting shot at or having to break into places or a lot of high-strung emotions. But if *Colibri Investigations* had been a wendek crime show like *Worra & Darith*, that case would never have been written as even a subplot in a script.

"Okay," Eddie said. "Your turn."

Alannah rolled her glass between her palms. "Hm, all right. Not in a million light years have I—" She stopped as their boss stepped into the galley. "Welcome back, Richard," she said instead.

"Thanks." He scanned the galley. "What are you two up to?"

"We're chatting and drinking Alannah's new iced black brew," Eddie said before Alannah had a chance to reply. "Want to taste?"

"Actually yes," Richard said and made a face. "I just had a cup that makes anything we have taste delicious."

Eddie handed him her glass, ignoring the way Alannah was trying to telepathically tell her to knock it off. It wasn't like she actually said anything.

"Thanks," Richard said and took a great, big mouthful. Then he slammed the glass onto the table before coughing racked his body. Tears filled his eyes, and he wheezed harder than the two of them had. "Alannah," he said when he regained control, "do you know any pilots looking for a job? I think I need to replace mine."

"Aw, come on," Eddie laughed. "It was too tempting. Besides, you'd have done the same to me."

"No," Richard said, "I most definitely would not."

"He's right. He wouldn't," Alannah agreed.

"You better watch your back," he said to Eddie and went to the other end of the galley to pour himself some water. "Why the hell are you drinking taarz in the first place?"

"We were playing not in a million light years," she replied.

Richard's eyebrows rose. "I haven't played that since I was a teenager."

"Here's your chance," Eddie said, making an expansive, inclusive gesture.

"No thanks. But if I'm interrupting your game, I suppose I shouldn't tell you about the job proposal."

Eddie snorted. "Oh, come on. Spill it."

Richard looked at them in turn to make sure they were actually listening. As if they couldn't easily switch from downtime-mode to work-mode. "All right," he finally began, "as I mentioned, my acquaintance is human and lives on Wenamak. The case she contacted me about is regarding a group of wendek arms dealers who supply other species illegally, primarily humans. They also have a few other questionable or criminal activities going on.

"And she wants us to stop it?" Eddie asked. Now, this was the kind of job she could get invested in.

"No. An associate of hers is the actual employer."

"And something about that worries you?" Alannah asked. Eddie had known Richard for longer than she had, but she was great at picking up on mood shifts and signs.

"Yes," Richard continued, inclining his head to acknowledge Alannah. "He is wendek. My friend was cryptic, but from what I can gather, he is in the peace corps or the security agency, and needs someone to expose the criminals by pretending to want to buy from them."

"I don't see the issue," Eddie said. It sounded straight-forward enough.

"It's the fact that he's wendek," Alannah said.

"Yes," Richard said again. "*Colibri* Investigations takes care of human interests because meddling with the rules of other species is delicate and complicated. I have arguments for and against taking on this one, but I want to know what you think."

"No problem," Eddie said, shrugging. "I don't care who hires us. Some people are doing some fucked up shit, we stop them. Doesn't matter if they're human or draever or wendek or whatever."

Alannah chewed her lip. "I am technically with Eddie here. But I think we need to know who the employer is. We need to be sure he has the proper credentials."

"That's my thought exactly," Richard agreed. "And he needs to have a solution to the smell concerns."

"He probably does if he is as competent as we hope," Alannah mused.

"Like smell-canceling perfume?" Eddie asked. "I thought that was only a plot device in wendek entertainment to make other species more mysterious."

"Oh, pheromone blockers do exist," Alannah explained, "but they aren't over-the-counter stuff."

"The Terran Defense Force has access to them," Richard added, "and I assume wendek authorities do too. Anyway, I want to do this as a favor to my friend, but I need to know whom I'll be working with." He glanced down at his patch. "I'm expecting a call from our mysterious wendek any moment. In the meantime... feel free to play on."

"You sure you don't want to join us?" Eddie asked, grinning.

It was only a few more rounds of not in a million light years before Richard returned to the galley looking like a man who was concealing how annoyed he really was.

"Not someone with the right credentials, then?" Alannah asked.

"That isn't the issue right now," Richard said. "Are you familiar with Space Arts & Crafts?"

"Oh yes," Alannah said. "They have some wonderful projects. I once took one of their zero G painting courses... Which," she added, "is not something you necessarily need to know."

"What about them?" Eddie asked. Everyone with wendek connections knew the company. It was super popular and catered to a number of demographics.

"We are invited to a meeting with our potential employer in one of their lounges."

"Really? A lounge? All of us?" Alannah asked, missing the point entirely, judging from the excited expression on her face.

"I told him I would bring my assistants," Richard said. "Because you two are much more used to wendek culture than I am, and you both speak the language. If I take the job, I will need you with me too, Eddie."

"Um," Alannah said, raising her hand for attention. "Eddie speaks Menal."

"Yes?" Richard said. "That is one of the reasons I want her to come along."

Eddie suppressed a snort. "Richard," she said, "Wenamak mostly uses Synal. I can read Synal, but listening to me trying to speak it is about as pleasant as being blown off course by hyperwind. Like, you're going somewhere, but it's clearly the wrong way."

"Whereas I grew up on Tewamak," Alannah said brightly. "Which means I'm fluent in Synal."

"I know," Richard replied. "But it might be dangerous, so Eddie's Menal will have to do."

"How about we go meet this mysterious stranger first and then decide?" Alannah asked.

"Yeah, right now we have a bigger problem," Eddie agreed. When the others looked blank, she added, "What do we wear?"

Lounge was synonymous with really fancy. Everybody with even the most basic knowledge of wendek culture knew that, and Eddie went to her cabin in search of something suitable. You could only store so much stuff on a small spaceship, and the printer had its limitations, which left her with pretty few options. But she did have one really nice outfit. Admittedly, it looked a lot like everything else she wore, but the fabric was more expensive, and the shirt was a gift from her sister, back when they were still on speaking terms. Eddie hadn't worn it for years, but since she had regained the muscle she had before she was fired from her old job and her life went out the airlock, it should fit. And, more importantly, it was wendek design.

She pinched the ribbon attached to the standing collar and wrapped it around her throat and into a knot that her wendek uncle had taught her. Tucked the shirt into the waistband of her pants and gave her own reflection a final look. She almost picked up her battered ecoleather jacket, but no. That was the definition of unfancy. Resigned, Eddie grabbed her nice jacket instead. It was too tight for comfort over her shoulders, but it wasn't like she expected to do any physical exercise.

When humans decided to name their spaceship types after bird species, shuttle craft were wittily nicknamed chicks and shuttle bays nests, and it was to the *Colibri*'s nest that Eddie was going now.

Richard was already there when she arrived. Eddie gave him an appraising look. There was this thing about Richard where he would always have a faint military look about him. A clean-cut, no-nonsense sort of air. But somehow he had managed to remove that effect today. His pants were loose with an asymmetric pleated front, and his shirt was a tight, sleeveless thing that revealed his, objectively speaking, very nice physique. He was also wearing jewelery and makeup if Eddie wasn't mistaken. A jacket matching his pants was draped over his arm.

"Hold on, didn't I see you in that episode of *Worra & Darith* with the human antagonist who ate zetoi eggs for shits and giggles?" Eddie said.

"Oh no. I've been found out," Richard replied, as deadpan as ever. He studied her and didn't bitch about her outfit, so he probably approved.

And then Alannah appeared.

"Damn," Eddie said with emphasis before she could stop herself.

Alannah was wearing a dress with a subtle floral pattern winding about her body in a way that would make any sane person wish they were a flower. It was cinched at her waist, wendek-style, and had a flattering cutout at her collarbones before it went on to a stylish clasp at her throat. She was wearing a light jacket over it that suggested it wasn't so much there to keep her from freezing as to add a little extra to the outfit. Her hair was done up in some sort of bun that allowed a few curly strands to escape and look purposely casual. She was also wearing bright blue earrings in a distinctly wendek design that contrasted her brown skin perfectly. Right to the top, but never over it.

"Too much?" Alannah said.

"No, you are perfect! For the job, I mean," Eddie added.

Alannah's smile widened.

"You look very convincing," Richard said. "Are the fathes real?"

Alannah's hand went to her earrings. "Yes. These were a birthday present from a geologist friend of my parents on Tewamak. I've had them for nearly a decade, but I rarely have a chance to wear them," she said.

"Nice," Eddie said, trying to look like she was talking about the earrings.

Q: *What kinds of activities do you offer?*

A: Space Crafts & Arts offers a broad selection of creative activities. Our main focus is on traditional wendek crafts and art such as reed weaving, wesh pigment painting and, the most popular activity offered, genao model paste sculpting.

 - Please refer to *Activities* for more information on all our offers.

Q: *What is the difference between a Workshop, a Lounge and a Course?*

A: A Workshop is an informal place to meet others and have fun with creative projects. If you want a fun and relaxed time with your friends or family, meet new people while engaging in your favorite creative hobby, or find others with whom to casually exchange feedback, a Workshop is the right choice for you. A Lounge provides a space for you to immerse yourself in the creation process alone or with a group of friends or colleagues. There is a wider variety in catering options as well as a selection of legal recreational vapors, and the comfort standard is both customizable and extremely high. A Course is, as the name suggests, an activity where a certified teacher is present to guide you through the creative process. Courses are available in both Workshops and Lounges. In Workshops, you can sign up for these classes with typically 10 to 30 other creatives, selecting a subject and level that fits your interests and experience. In Lounges, Courses are tailored to the individual or group of less than 15 people, and top-tier professional quality tools and materials are provided. In both locations, you are able to choose between a purely practical approach and a Course that also spiritually guides you and helps you open your mind to the healing effects of creation.

Q: *Can I book a private room for my friends and me?*

A: All of our Workshops have a large room for everybody to mingle and enjoy their creativity together, as well as smaller rooms for different types of crafts and art and Courses. For a more intimate or private setting to explore your creativity, you can book a space in our Lounges.

Q: *What is the dress code for the different venues?*

A: Our Workshops have no requirements (apart from following the same common decency rules as the rest of society). In our Lounges, however, we ask that you dress semi-formally (please note that we have no restrictions based on gender or culture).

Q: *Do you accept non-wendek visitors?*

A: Yes, we do. Creative pursuits should be for everybody! In fact, our Courses are very popular among åayu, humans and many other species. Our staff is fluent in Standard as well as the respective locations' predominant languages. All we ask is that persons of other species follow the local rules and regulations and adhere to the dresscode as indicated above.

— Excerpt from the official Space Crafts & Arts FAQ

3

GETTING CREATIVE

Alannah was in her element. She had been beaming all the way from the chick port to the most posh part of Kwipadam where the Space Crafts & Arts Lounge was located. The building was tall and with a design that struck Richard as oddly incongruous, but which, according to Alannah's enthusiastic explanation, was a perfect merge of traditional wendek architecture and a modern, high tech and environmentally responsible style. It was not only her normal travel guide mode. She grew up on a wendek planet, and everything that Richard had to process, she automatically understood.

Now Alannah practically bounced ahead of Richard and Eddie to approach the reception desk and greet the staff person in flawless Synal. It made as much sense to Richard as any other language he heard, which was none at all.

Next to him, Eddie smiled, and Richard didn't know if it was pride in Alannah or if Alannah had said something funny that Eddie's Synal vocabulary was sufficient to catch.

Alannah beckoned them closer. "Our friend is already here," she said in Standard, and Richard quickly recalibrated his brain to

Standard phonetics and syntax. In private, the three of them usually spoke English, but this was more polite in front of someone who wasn't likely to know any human languages.

"I will let him know you are here. Please go ahead," the staff member said, also in Standard.

Alannah said something that was probably a thank you in Synal. Eddie and Richard echoed the sentiment in Standard and hurried up to catch up to Alannah who was already moving.

She was heading for an elevator, a big plass cage with beautiful inlaid colored panes that reflected the light filtering in through the transparent ceiling above. A sign projected above them in midair changed between Synal, Menal and Standard. "Welcome to Space Crafts & Art!" it read.

They entered the elevator, and Alannah told it which floor they needed to go to. Richard didn't mind her taking charge of this part. The elevator rose, treating them to a lovely view of the spacious lobby area. When it stopped, they found themselves emerging into a corridor with all kinds of artworks hanging on and lining the walls. The products of visitors to this place, or pretending to be? They weren't the sort of thing hobbyists created. Probably. Richard didn't know much about wendek art.

Alannah stopped a few paces down the corridor. "Second door on your right," she told Richard.

"Thank you." Richard made his way to the transparent door. It opened up to a colorfully decorated room with small statuettes displayed on shelves. A faint, pleasant smell wafted from a censer, and Richard had no doubt that a wendek nose would be able to pick up a lot more from it than just a nice odor. Four cups and a pot on a heating pad were sitting on the low table in the middle of the room, and a basket had been placed next to the floor cushion by each of them. Their potential client rose from one of these cushions when they entered.

"Richard, Alannah, Eddie!" he greeted them warmly, "It's so good to see you again!"

"Hello, Raithan," Richard said. So the wendek was going to pretend they already knew each other.

Their host touched his patch, and the door became opaque as it closed behind them. Next, he took off his patch and placed it on the table. "Now we have some privacy," he said and reached out to shake each of their hands in the standard human greeting. "Thank you for coming."

Alannah, not about to be outdone by anyone's knowledge of another culture's customs, held both hands in front of her, palms up, bowed over them and spoke a few words.

Raithan mimicked her greeting and said something that made Alannah attempt not to look like she wanted to laugh.

"Alannah's Synal is better than mine," Raithan said in Standard with a brilliant smile. "My native language is Menal. Please, have a seat." He folded himself up as gracefully as a cat or a dancer. Wendek were considered attractive by all category 3 species in the Union, somehow hitting the right marks of the other species in a Venn's diagram of beauty. Raithan was no exception. He was slender and tall with long, graceful limbs. His large eyes were a stunning reddish amber, and his skin a warm shade of dark grey that would probably look almost bronze in the right light. His long hair was dyed blue and tied back in an elaborate hairstyle. And he was, of course, wearing a semi-formal wendek attire with a broad sash cinching his waist and layers upon layers of thin fabric. "Thank you for agreeing to see me," he continued. "Twa?"

"Please," Alannah said.

"What flavor?" Eddie asked and then, perhaps sensing that Richard was about to give her a stern look for lack of politeness, added, "I have a mild allergy to quai berries."

"Ah, this is mynth," Raithan said.

"Oh, good. In that case, thank you," Eddie said, allowing the wendek to pour.

Richard held up his cup too, trying to mentally prepare himself for the conversation ahead as well as the twa. Mynth never stopped surprising him, simply for the fact that it sounded a lot like a human herb and tasted completely different.

"You did not mention whom you are working for," Richard said. Better get that detail out of the way as soon as possible.

"No, I didn't," Raithan said. There was an awkward stretch of silence.

"I am going to need some credentials before I agree to work with you," Richard elaborated.

"Of course you are," Raithan said with a small twitch of his nostrils that might convey annoyance to someone fluent in wendek mannerisms. "I am Raithan WeinZalneinth, first class independent agent of the Federal Wendek Security Agency." He reached into his robe and retrieved a coin-sized metal disc, sketched a pattern on its surface with his finger and held it out for inspection as a projection faded into view. It was a rotating depiction of the logo of the FWSA on one side and Raithan's name and still on the other.

"Thank you," Richard said. He had only seen a FWSA identifier once before, but he knew they were nearly impossible to fake.

"I will get right to the point, then," Raithan continued after raising his cup in a quiet toast. There was something about him that reminded Richard of another client of his. Probably, it was the smooth ease and absolute confidence with which Raithan spoke, the elegant way he carried himself and his above average, even for a wendek, good looks. Perhaps, Richard mused, every military intelligence department and secret service had a Micah Dietrich. If so, this was clearly the wendek version.

"In short, a local gang is illegally supplying groups of other species, mainly humans and draevere, with weapons. The Kwipadam peace corps' interspecies affairs department has not put a stop to it.

In fact, they claim to not only lack evidence but also be unaware that anything of the sort is going on. My job is to stop the weapon trade and find out whether there is any underlying reason for their inability to acquire proof."

Richard made a noise of agreement. Raithan was looking for corruption and blackmail of the authorities in Kwipadam, in other words.

"The same group runs an underground fighting ring specializing in the novelty of fighters of other species," Raithan went on. "While it is not my primary priority to stop that, I would very much like to add that to the charges." He indicated the baskets arranged around the table. "Please help yourselves. Get creative."

"Pardon?" Richard asked.

Raithan had already opened up his own basket and was taking out a white substance that looked remarkably like clay. "Please help yourselves," he repeated, enunciating the words more clearly.

Richard glanced around at his crew.

"I don't really do genao sculpting," Eddie said.

Alannah already had her own white lump out and was separating it into two portions. A mildly disapproving expression appeared on her face when she saw her companions not diving into whatever it was that they were supposed to do.

"Perhaps we should get on with the meeting?" Richard suggested.

"We can talk and sculpt at the same time," Raithan said. "You are going to take the job, yes?"

"There are a few things we need to address, but unless I am mistaken regarding what the job entails, yes," Richard agreed.

"Very well. Please consider sculpting something with genao model paste the first task of the mission," Raithan said. His long fingers were kneading the paste even as he spoke. "I invited you here in order for our meeting to appear inconspicuous. A person in my position has to be very careful, as you no doubt are aware. And not producing anything in a place like this is a little conspicuous, wouldn't you say?"

Richard tried to picture Colonel Dietrich insisting on having a hobby session and found that, disturbingly, that was exactly the kind of thing they would do in the interest of keeping things clandestine, should the need arise. He opened his basket.

"Sculpting is a meditative pastime," Alannah said. "It's very popular in most wendek communities. Genao model paste resembles clay, but it is less messy." She held up a clean hand to demonstrate. "I haven't done this for quite a while, though, so don't judge my syraxh, all right?"

"It already looks like a syraxh!" Eddie said, amazed.

Richard agreed. The lump on the table had pointy ears and a short snout at this point. "Fine," Richard said. "Eddie, get sculpting."

"Oh, come on!" Eddie protested. "Alannah likes it. She can have my paste."

"I would vastly prefer it if you all participated," Raithan said.

Richard squeezed the lump he had picked up. It was cool and squishy and dry to the touch and surprisingly comfortable to close your fingers around.

Eddie reluctantly picked up her own model paste and began to poke at it.

"So," Raithan carried on as if the little intermezzo had never taken place, "I would like to stop both of their illegal activities at the same time and unravel the whole power structure of the gang. Being human, you are the perfect candidates to strike a weapon deal with them. A cursory background check on you reveals nothing that would set them off, and I daresay you have some expertise in weapons."

"Yes," Richard simply said. He certainly did. Eddie too, to some extent.

"All you need to do is approach them and arrange a meeting to negotiate and inspect the goods. I want you to play along, set up a time and a place for the transaction itself, and then I will take it from there. I will provide you with enough units to pay a substantial deposit, of course." Raithan paused to look down at his figure and smooth out the paste here and there.

"How are you planning on circumventing the pheromonic aspects?" Richard asked. That wasn't really a word in English, but it was in Standard.

"Pheromone blockers with... shall we say a little extra?" Raithan said.

"Please define a little extra." Richard's paste was suffering from him having to lipread instead of looking at it, but there was nothing to be done about that.

"My assistant has devised a variation with a little bit of perfume and a little bit of honesty. They have a background in chemistry," Raithan said by way of explanation. "Now, as for the fighting ring, evidence will do. The audience is mostly wendek, so I will go myself, but it is a two person job, and I would like the diversion of bringing a human."

"How so?" Richard asked. "One person can take a still or record a clip."

"True," Raithan said, "and I have tried that, of course. But they have a media privacy filter set up that renders any recording incomprehensible and unusable. There is a way around that, but a simple descrambler would be detected immediately by security. As it happens, I have a device that consists of two components, each looking inoffensive on its own. So all I need is for one of you to go to a fight with me and casually hand me one of the components at an opportune moment. Straight forward."

Richard knew that technique from doing surveillance in his former career in military intelligence. "All right. Eddie, are you up for that?" he asked.

"Sure. It sounds simple enough," she replied with a shrug. Eddie's paste was now ball-shaped and with an indent in the middle. She was pulling at it to create a vase or a jar.

"And I will negotiate for the weapons," Richard said.

"With me," Alannah added.

"Alannah, it's not safe," Richard emphasized.

Alannah pursed her lips. "Come on, Richard. We have been over this. You'll want someone who's fluent in Synal with you. I'm not going to suddenly blow your cover."

Yes, he had agreed he wanted someone fluent in Synal with him today. Not that he wanted to bring her on the actual job. Maybe if he brought Eddie instead... But that would leave Alannah with Raithan, and even if it ought to be safe, complications could always arise. She did not have the experience with these things that Eddie did.

Richard looked at Eddie.

"If she gets hurt, I will kill you," his pilot said with a smile that was all teeth and warning.

Raithan glanced from one to the other. His hands had gone completely still on the figure in front of him, and Richard saw him breathe in, no doubt taking in smells that the three of them could not pick up on. "Fascinating," he said.

Richard wondered what the man was discerning from their pheromones. "It's a figure of speech," he reassured him.

There was nothing reassuring about Eddie's expression.

Richard cleared his throat. "All right, Alannah. I will bring you along when we approach them the first time. That should not involve any danger."

"Deal," Alannah said.

"So, I assume you have a lead for us on how to get in contact with these people?" Richard asked Raithan.

The wendek's fingers left the model paste and touched his patch. "Of course. I'll send you the relevant information and stills of some of the key players as well as my contingency plan in case of unforeseen complications. I'm querying for a private connection."

Richard accepted. He didn't ask if it was secure because that would be an insult. A handful of files appeared on his patch.

"Your decryption password is a numerical string. I expect you can memorize it?"

"Go ahead," Richard said, though he would much rather have it in writing than lipreading it.

Raithan surprised him by raising his hands and signing the code in Standard sign language. 07030904184881.

"Got it," Richard told him.

"Eddie," Raithan resumed speaking. "Are you free tomorrow night?"

"Um, yeah?" she said.

"We should meet up for a drink, then." Apparently not sure Eddie was getting the point, he added, "to get invitations for the fighting ring."

"Oh. Right. Sure."

"I'll send you the location and time," Raithan said. "Alannah, that is lovely."

Richard looked down at the figure on the table in front of Alannah. The syraxh had a ridiculous amount of detail now. Even the wings looked realistic.

"Thank you," Alannah said, beaming.

Raithan's own figure, a curvy person whose proportions looked more human than wendek, was every bit as good. Eddie had indeed made a vase, wobbly, but not that bad for someone who didn't enjoy the hobby. Richard's own project... Well, he had made a snowman, and a five year old wendek child could probably have done it better.

Raithan's preliminary intel suggested one particular location as the site for signing up as a fighter or procuring invitations to watch the matches in the underground fighting ring. But a quick reconnaissance of the premises was needed, and it would be suspicious if the same person showed up in the same place twice. So it was time for my own, albeit brief as is often the case, public performance.

When I escaped the unpleasantly humid evening air of Kwipadam, it was into a mixed species establishment where less than a fourth of the patrons were wendek. The rest consisted mostly of humans and draevere, but I spotted two groups of zetois as well. The lack of åayu was probably a hint as to what sort of place this was.

I approached the bar and, having instructions to blend in, had to order a drink and not vapor. Luckily, an item intrigued me immediately, and I would have ordered it regardless of whether I was meant to or not. It was called Irish black brew and was an alcoholic twist of the traditional human beverage with an addition of sweetener. The human bartender found my fascination amusing and confided in me which alcohol was used. I will definitely be conducting experiments of my own to create such a drink.

But I digress. The smells in the room were poignant even to my nose. As a precaution, I was wearing the pheromone blockers I devised for Raithan, and you can imagine my amusement when the human bartender complimented my perfume. After lingering at the bar for a while, I managed to strike up conversation with the least intimidating draever I could spot. He was only a head taller than I and though muscular, he was no more bulky than a large human. I told him I have a draever friend, which is not too far from the truth as I am still in contact with one of the exchange students from my time at the Institute of Science on Ganmak. The draever was talkative enough, especially when I bought him a drink. So I asked him if he had been on Wenamak for long, if he had family here, that sort of thing. I also casually asked him what he did for a living, and I did not need to be able to smell the signs to detect that it brought up his defenses immediately. He murmured something about spotting a friend further back in the establishment, clearly an excuse to leave, but emboldened by my acquaintance with the Irish black brew, I acted on my hunch and leaned in, looking him in the eyes as only a draever who is trying to pick a fight or a bed partner would do. I told him I had heard rumors. Nothing else.

The draever studied me, then told me I had better ask the staff if I had the units to back up my enthusiasm before he left.

When I returned to our temporary base of operations, Raithan was already back and, admittedly, more sober than I.

— Kellieth ReinAraneinth's private journal

4
A WIN-WEN SITUATION

Over the years, Alannah had visited restaurants and bars that people in all walks of life went to. And she did mean all. How was she expected to write about the seedy, dangerous places that tourists should avoid if she didn't actually go there to verify?

The same philosophy accounted for why she had sipped cocktails with umbrellas in them on beaches with rainbow-colored sand and tasted all kinds of delicacies that she would never have been able to afford without the sponsorship of a traveling agency. Travel guide writing was about authenticity, and authenticity was all about getting a taste of real life.

Today's restaurant was one of the fancy ones. When Eddie had dressed down for her appointment with Raithan, Alannah and Richard had dressed up again today.

Their plan was simple, but Richard had made her go over it twice. She had played along. If he needed the reassurance that she knew what they were doing, who was she to take that security blanket away?

Flagging down a rent ride on a wendek planet used to be a hassle if you belonged to one of the smellier species in the galaxy, but the tourism industry in Kwipadam ensured that rent drivers had nose plugs or a facemask readily available or had partitioned the transport so that no odors would permeate the air they breathed.

"Hello," Alannah greeted the rent driver as their groundwheeler slid sideways to stop by the spot where she and Richard were waiting and opened the back hatch of the vehicle. "If you are free, we would like a ride to Syrelo Square."

"Good evening. Hop right in," the driver said, looking at them in the rear view display.

Alannah slipped in and arranged her dress while Richard got in next to her. Wendek rent ride vehicles were comfortable and had wider seats and more leg room than private ones in order to accommodate broader species or simply more people, and this was no exception.

"Your Synal is amazing," the driver said as they slid back into the traffic.

"Thank you," Alannah replied with a practiced smile. "I grew up on Tewamak." She was always half flattered and half annoyed when people complimented her Synal. Because of course she spoke it fluently. It felt awkward to be greeted with surprise and awe at something she had done practically all her life. But at the same time, that wasn't fair to the person giving her the compliment. It wasn't like she had a tag on her saying, "Grew up speaking Synal; please don't be surprised."

Alannah shot Richard a glance. Maybe she should switch to Standard.

"No, it's fine," he said in Standard as if reading her thoughts.

"Your friend doesn't speak Synal, then?" the driver asked.

"No, he doesn't," Alannah replied. In fact, that was the reason she was here right now.

"So, are you here for business or pleasure?"

"A bit of both," Alannah said automatically. It was her standard response as a travel guide writer. "Mostly business," she added. She smoothed out the fabric of her dress again though it didn't need it. She had to admit she was a little nervous. Not scared. Just slightly apprehensive. Raithan hadn't specified how he knew that the arms dealers would be in the restaurant in Syrelo Square tonight, but he must have been staking out and gathering intel on the group for quite a while.

They quickly arrived at the square, and Alannah paid for the ride. Prior to going out, Richard had horrified her by asking how much he ought to tip the driver, and she had decided to take over all their transactions tonight. Tipping was an insult here. Rating a service on the local PlaNet's primary business portal, Win-Wen, was not. "Thank you for the ride," Alannah said and swiped at her patch. The driver's name and a still of them showed up immediately on Win-Wen. "Seven protheran stars," she announced. The highest rating possible. She set her standards lower than the average wendek who would rarely fork over a top score unless something overwhelmingly fantastic had happened, but Alannah couldn't see how a short ride in a rent driver's groundwheeler could possibly be overwhelmingly fantastic, and she did not believe in punishing people for their choice of career.

"Thank you," the driver said, clearly pleased.

Richard got out first and offered Alannah his hand for support as she climbed out of the groundwheeler. "Any last minute questions?" he asked.

"No," Alannah said. "You?"

Richard raised an eyebrow as if that was unthinkable.

They approached the entrance to the restaurant where a guard was standing like she was on a military exercise.

"We have a reservation," Richard said without any preamble and held out his wrist. The guard scanned his patch.

"Please go right in, sir," the guard replied.

The doors slid open on a dimly lit and extremely beautiful, if a little overdone, space. Chandeliers, soft music and softer carpet, more white than you normally found in wendek interior decoration, and tasteful, unintrusive art on the walls. Alannah kept her face straight. Now was not the time to gawk even if her fingers itched to take a few stills for later scrutiny.

Heads turned. They were the only humans in this place, and Alannah knew that as uncomfortable as it felt, the patrons were noticing them not because of their looks, but because of the way they smelled. They had both showered and brushed their teeth right before leaving the *Colibri*, and they had made sure to use effective antiperspirant without any strong added odors along with Raithan's pheromone blockers. But they were still human.

"Welcome to Syrelo Supreme. Do you have a reservation?" asked the waiter approaching them, even though he must know the guard outside already checked.

"Yes," Richard said and held out his arm to have his patch scanned once more.

"Very good. Please follow me to your table."

They did. The wendek at the various tables tried to look like they were not noticing the humans among them, and Alannah tried to look like she wasn't trying to figure out whom they were here to meet.

They were seated at a table in the far end of the room, close to the section reserved for private parties that every high-end wendek establishment had.

"Please take your time to order. Would you like a drink while you wait?"

Richard studied the bar where a couple of patrons were chatting while waiting for their drinks. "Mind if I head up there and look at what you have? I prefer seeing how my drinks are made."

Alannah wondered at the request, but then she realized what Richard had seen. One of the people at the bar matched the stills of one of the weapons dealers Raithan had showed them. "Go ahead, sweetie," she said to Richard. "You know what I like. If you get drinks to start us off, I will have a look at the menu."

Richard squeezed her shoulder affectionately, something he never usually did. But then, she never called him sweetie, either. "I'll be right back."

Alannah smiled at him in a way that she hoped conveyed he'd better get her something really fancy that she would normally never splurge on since Raithan was paying.

As Richard made his way to the bar and the waiter went to greet another group at the entrance, Alannah began to study the menu. She nearly wept with joy. So many delicacies she knew from her childhood, specific to certain parts of the wendek culture. Every settlement had its own twist, of course, but reading the menu brought back fond memories. She decided on a selection of small dishes as the first course and happily ignored the pricetag. She had not been able to do that for quite some time. Back when she had been one of the top writers for Starlite Planetary Guides, the company would often sponsor her eating exquisite meals, but that was not something she or *Colibri* Investigations could afford.

Alannah glanced up. Richard was pointing at something. The bartender made an affirmative gesture and began to take out the ingredients. And Richard turned back to check up on Alannah. No, he turned back pretending to check up on her, but it was to catch the attention of one of the people at the bar. Alannah couldn't hear what they were saying, but she could tell Richard was communicating with him.

"Here you go," he said when he returned and put down two drinks on the table between them. "One Vermillion Sunset for you."

"Oooh," Alannah cooed. "Thank you." He had gotten the message and made sure she got something super fancy. It was not an alcoholic beverage. They did exist, but wendek generally preferred their intoxication in other shapes. "And yours is a Golden Anish?"

"Indeed," he replied.

"I noticed you talked to the guy up there?" she continued.

"Yes. We seem to have similar interests. He invited us to meet him and his friends after we have eaten. They are in one of the private rooms," Richard said.

"That was quick. You are good," Alannah said, smiling.

"Yes," Richard agreed, which was slightly out of character for him but fit the role he was performing tonight splendidly.

Alannah would have liked to enjoy the dishes with every fiber of her body, but when the food was served, she could not help eating a little too fast and a little too mechanically. It wasn't fair to her tastebuds, but she was a bit jittery. Richard did not appear particularly weighed down, but he was more used to this kind of thing.

After they had enjoyed, or tried to enjoy, the dessert, Richard asked for Alannah's advice on what to bring with them to the private room. "Unless a gift is as much of a faux pas as tipping," he added in an undertone.

"It's not," Alannah said, appreciating that he had thought of it. "I'd go with mild and exclusive vapor. Do you know how many people we're going to see?"

"No," Richard said. "It sounded like maybe a handful."

"Get 12 vials, then. You want to appear generous."

Richard followed her instructions and bought a frame with 12 vials set into it, the price of which was roughly the equivalent of what Alannah made in a month. "Are these safe for humans?" he asked her as they made their way to the private room.

"Yes," Alannah said. "Think of each as... half a unit of alcohol."

Inside, five people clearly had finished their dinner. There was a vague scent of vapors already, but a look at the empty vials on the table revealed that they had not been indulging in anything as expensive as what Richard was carrying. Nice.

"Ah, Richard, glad you could make it," the man Richard had talked to at the bar said in Standard. As if they might not have.

"Of course. I hope you like this," Richard replied, handing over the frame.

The wendek made a show of looking appreciatively at it. Colorful mist swirled around inside the vials. And then he looked appreciatively at Alannah. "And who is your lovely companion?" he asked in a way that spelled creep in any cat 3 society. Wendek sleazeballs could be dangerous because one instantly tended to find any wendek charming, but Alannah had a lifetime of experience in figuring out what was their innate attractiveness and what was genuine friendliness. She smiled and did what she hoped looked like a stiff amateur version of the same greeting she had given Raithan. They had agreed it was better to keep her intimate knowledge of wendek customs and languages secret for now. "My name is Alannah," she said, also in Standard.

"Come, have a seat. I am Lejja," the man said and indicated each of his companions, introducing them in turn. "So," he continued, "What is it that we can do for you? Don't be shy."

Richard looked up, searching the ceiling with his gaze. He was making sure there was no surveillance in here, Alannah realized. Apparently satisfied, Richard returned his attention to Lejja. "We are looking for some firepower. Something effective. As discreet as possible."

"Hmm," Lejja replied. "And how much are we talking?"

"We're in the market to arm a dozen or twenty people. All humans," Richard said without hesitation.

Lejja looked thoughtful. "A small operation, then. That should not be a problem."

A small operation. It sounded like a pretty big deal to Alannah. She hadn't imagined anything on a scale that made arming twenty people trivial. But then, would a FWSA agent be involved if it was any smaller than this?

"And I am specifically looking for something hard to track," Richard continued.

Lejja smiled. "A few things come to mind. I think we have exactly what you need. When do you need the goods to be ready?"

"As soon as possible. I'm on a tight schedule. I trust you don't need to hear the details?" Richard said.

Lejja tapped the air with two fingers. "The less we know about each other, the better, wouldn't you say? Now, I am not in charge, but I can set you up for a meeting in a couple of days and you can make a deal with my boss. How does that sound?"

"That sounds good," Richard said. "All I need is a location and a time, and I will be there."

Lejja shifted his attention to Alannah. "Will you be there too?" he asked.

"If Richard wants me to," Alannah replied. She wasn't sure if Richard actually wanted her there. She wasn't sure she wanted her there.

"I hope he does," Lejja said.

Alannah thought she caught a fleeting look of irritation on Richard's face. "She's my good luck charm," he replied without any hint of the annoyance in his voice. "I'm going to need to sample the goods before we finalize anything."

"Of course," Lejja said. "I will be in touch. Now, a toast. Like you humans do." He made a gesture to one of the others who promptly picked three vials from the frame Richard had brought and handed them one each.

"To our future cooperation!" Lejja raised his vial expectantly.

Richard raised his too, accepting the toast. Alannah hadn't instructed him in how to breathe in the vial's contents properly, but she trusted he had watched enough wendek entertainment to have the general idea.

"To the future," Alannah said, smiling and meaning something completely different.

human4lyfe: I cant find the post someone made about the fighting ring in
    Kwipadam
Frewerath: No idea what you're talking about.
NIHILS: same
Irb56000: What fighting ring? Got clips?
human4lyfe: That place where they have aliens beat up each other
human4lyfe: No clips. Someone posted about going a while back. There's a
    human with wicked prosthetics fighting draevere and all sorts of
    crazy shit like that
NIHILS: @human4lyfe stop asking about the fighting ring on the main
    forum!! The post you mentioned got deleted
human4lyfe: @NIHILS why???
NIHILS: @human4lyfe u dont mention it thats why. Its not exactly "legal"
    and u never know who is listening in on a public board
NIHILS: @human4lyfe besides u cant just go there dimdek
human4lyfe: @NIHILS why not??
NIHILS: @human4lyfe u gotta know the right people to get an invitation
human4lyfe: @NIHILS do YOU know the right ppl???

[Message could not be delivered.]

human4lyfe: @NIHILS dude did you block me or smthng???

[Message could not be delivered.]

— Discussion on Wenamak PlaNet

5

INVITES ONLY

Raithan looked splendid because he was wendek and a wendek could put on a garbage disposal bag and poke holes for their head and arms and still look fabulous. Well, fabulous but really weird.

"Yes?" Raithan said in Menal. "Is there anything you want to ask?"

Eddie wiped the beginning of a grin at the thought of a wendek in a garbage bag off her face. "Um, no. I'm good," she replied, also in Menal.

Raithan sized her up. "You look the part," he said.

"Thanks," she replied. "You too."

He acknowledged this with a small inclination of his head, making the small braids of today's hairdo bounce a bit. He was wearing white, which was the most impractical color available to the spectrum of both human and wendek perception. But in wendek society especially, it signaled that this was someone who was not expecting to have to get down and dirty. Ever.

According to Raithan's instructions, Eddie had dressed up as herself. He hadn't specifically told her to dress up as herself, of course, but the instructions to "look like a bodyguard, someone armed and a bit rough around the edges and with a challenging glare" felt suspiciously close to her normal self. Eddie had decided to emphasize it a bit by adding a few props.

She normally did carry a weapon or two. It made sense when working with Richard. Authority could be a great many things, but one of the easiest ways to convey the fact that you were serious about your job as a private investigator was to have a dart gun holstered at your side as a warning. Eddie's Union weapon license was in order. She could legally carry dart guns in most places in the galaxy as long as they didn't contain any lethal darts. Today, she had fastened her customary holster to her belt, and then found an extra belt to loop around her waist for her favorite gun which happened to be too stupid to lug around on a regular basis. It was old and scuffed and heavy as fuck, and it had useless adornments consisting of inlaid semi-precious wendek gemstones. It was a gift from her wendek uncle who had pissed off practically Eddie's entire family, including his own spouse, but delighted teenage Eddie to no ends. Giving a kid a gun did sound like an extremely bad idea, but all of its potentially dangerous innards were missing. Anyway, now the gun wasn't useless anymore. A few years ago, Eddie had it retrofitted with a working mechanism making it a legal dart gun. And it was beautiful. True to wendek aesthetics, its holster was a revealing mesh so anyone could admire the piece.

"That is a beautiful antique," Raithan added.

"Thank you," Eddie said. It was nice that someone appreciated it. "Maybe I will let you touch it later."

"I should very much like that," he replied. "Well, let's make an entrance."

By which he meant sweep up to the door with inlaid mirrors and wait for it to open. It didn't.

Eddie pushed it open with the palm of her hand because it was an old fashioned door that relied on brute force. You could tell a lot about people and places from the kind of doors they kept. There was no need to discuss this one further. The picture was clear, unlike that in the grimy, cracked surface of said door.

"Ah," Raithan said as if it had never occurred to him to work a manual door. Eddie hoped that was part of his role today. Rich, dumb wendek looking for entertainment.

Noise exploded around them the instant they entered. Hard and fast draever music blared out of the speakers, a slight static feedback overlaying it. An attempt to mimic more old-fashioned means of music replay to match the door, or an actual ancient sound system? The decor was dated, too. Posters with draever bands that were already in decline when Eddie was a teen. A few political posters in Synal. A screen looping a menu.

Eddie assessed the occupants of the room. She leaned in for Raithan to be able to hear her. "Do you really think this place is suitable?" she asked, switching to Standard. Even if no one in the vicinity was able to overhear them, you never knew who was lipreading or recording everything. It was better to overact than underact.

Raithan looked down his perfect nose at her. "It's fantastic! Just find us a table and flag down a waiter," he said, also in Standard.

"Over there," Eddie said, taking point and pushing her way past a couple of humans. One of them looked like he wanted to punch her for it and the other rolled her eyes. Both were clearly intoxicated.

If someone had asked Eddie what a private investigator did before Richard hired her, she would have assumed meeting people or looking for information in drinking establishments across the galaxy was a dumb cliche. Someone who didn't know how to write a good detective show would set that kind of bar as the scene for information gathering based on a vague idea of how investigating actually worked and throw in a couple of bar fights for good, entertaining measure. But the fact was that she and Richard had spent a disturbingly huge amount of time in bars.

Raithan sat down at the table Eddie picked and adjusted the cuffs of his sleeves. He was breathing through his mouth now and trying to keep a look of disgust off his face. Eddie had no idea if that was for show too, but probably not. The place didn't exactly smell like flowers to her, and she wasn't picking up on even a fraction of the odors a wendek would. The clientele was mainly human and draever in here. It was an old joke that human sweat could make a wendek gag and their eyes water, but it was not unfounded. Eddie wondered why Raithan didn't put on a mask, but now wasn't the time to bring that up.

"I'm going to get us a drink. What do you want?" she asked. "Or should I ask for vapors for you?"

"No, a drink sounds good. I want the full experience," Raithan said. "Surprise me."

"Okay. Just don't get into trouble while I'm ordering," she told him, hoping that he would. Or not trouble, as such. But he should be able to attract the right kind of attention. She shot a look over her shoulder as she melted into the crowd closer to the bar. He was definitely standing out.

Eddie pushed through the narrow space between two draevere at the bar and waved at the bartender for attention. They were human, possibly of Chinese decent, younger than Eddie and with a thick, black braid of hair spilling down their back. They acknowledged Eddie with a nod as they passed her with a couple of glasses for two other humans at the far end of the bar.

It took a small eternity before it was Eddie's turn. She looked back over her shoulder to check up on Raithan a few times. The first time, he looked like he was trying to get eye contact with a human patron across the room. The second time, a draever a head taller and two heads wider than him was making her way to his table.

"Hey. Did you want to order?" the bartender said in Standard.

"Sorry, yeah," Eddie replied. "Anything you recommend?"

The bartender looked past Eddie and then back at her. "You ordering for your rich wendek boyfriend too?"

"No. I mean yes. I mean, yes I am ordering for both of us, but no he is not my boyfriend."

The bartender shrugged. "Okay then. Just, most wendek who come here are either with an alien or looking to pick up one, if you know what I mean."

This was a great opening. Eddie leaned forward, "I mean, he does have a thing for other species, but mostly draevere. I took him here so he could meet some. But mostly, he likes to watch. He's got this weird kink."

"Weird kink?" the bartender encouraged her, also leaning in and sounding conspiratorial.

"He likes watching draevere fight," Eddie fake-confided. "But I mean, whatever. He pays for my drinks, and I hook him up." This was totally not in the script, but Eddie felt a spark of inspiration and went with it. If this was where people got an invitation to the fighting ring, chances were the staff might know about it. "So let me know if you have any tips?"

The bartender's lips curved into a smile. "Two glasses of daazac, then? Do you?"

"Do I what?"

"Have any tips? I'm not wendek."

Oh, so that's how it went. "Two glasses of daazac sounds great," Eddie agreed. It didn't, actually, because no one but draevere enjoyed it. But it went well with the story about Raithan's draever kink. "I always tip when the service is good."

"I'm Percie," the bartender said. "105 units for the drinks."

"Coming right up," Eddie said and found the bar and Percie's name on the tab under it on her patch. She transferred 500 units, hoping that was appropriate. She wasn't going to ask. If it was not enough, she would get back up later, order another drink and repeat the whole thing.

Percie had their back to Eddie by now, but they glanced at their patch as the transfer popped up. Then they returned with the drinks. "Here you go. This is our best daazac," they said. "Stick around for a while, okay?"

"Sure. Thanks," Eddie replied, picked up the glasses and turned around.

The draever Raithan had tried to attract earlier was now sitting on the stool Eddie had expected to be hers. Raithan was staring at her with a rapt sort of expression, like a teenager in love.

"Eddie, meet my new friend!" Raithan said with bubbly excitement. "Her name is Tain— Tainteth..?" he tried. A classic Menal mispronunciation of a Draspaarg name, whether it was on purpose or not.

"Taantesh," the draever corrected his pronunciation.

"Yeah, hi, nice to meet you," Eddie said without great enthusiasm. "Here's your drink, Raithan," she added in Menal, since it fit her role to be a bit more rude than she usually was.

He took it. "Thank you," he said, sticking to Standard. "What is it?"

"Daazac," Eddie said.

For a short, fleeting instant, a look of horror passed Raithan's features. He managed to change it into excitement. "I love draever drinks!"

"Should I get another stool, or are you on your way back to your own friends?" Eddie asked Taantesh.

Taantesh sized her up. "Don't worry, I'm not about to steal your boyfriend."

"He's not—" Eddie groaned.

Raithan positively giggled.

"Anyway, I have to go. Early day tomorrow," Taantesh said and stood. She bent down to Raithan's eye level. "Wish me luck."

Raithan reached out and, to Eddie's utter surprise, pulled in the draever for a passionate kiss. "For luck," he said when they parted.

Eddie sat down on the vacated stool. She knew she was staring at Raithan in disbelief, and since he had not informed her that sticking his tongue down the throat of random people was part of the plan, she saw no reason to conceal it.

"Yes?" Raithan asked and picked up the glass Eddie had placed in front of him.

"Just wasn't expecting that," she said.

Raithan smiled and raised his glass to her.

Eddie took a sip of hers, watching Raithan doing the same. She barely avoided choking on it. He wasn't.

"Be careful with that," a new voice said in Standard. A wendek woman had crept up on them while they were busy not dying from draever alcohol. She was less striking than Raithan, her hair dyed but not styled very well, and her clothes were not at all flamboyant. She pulled up a stool and sat down at their table as if she owned the place. "I haven't seen you around before," she said.

"It's our first time here. A friend told us about the establishment," Raithan said, looking at her in a far less hungry way than he had the draever.

"I'm Chynna. I own this place," the woman said, which explained why she acted like she owned the place. "I hear you were asking about a certain type of entertainment."

Eddie gave her a slow, cunning smile.

"So you want to fight your own kind or be fresh meat for the draevere?" Chynna asked Eddie.

Eddie opened her mouth and closed it again on the two first things that came to mind. One, that sounded absolutely disgusting. Two, Raithan was clearly the one into draevere.

"She's my friend," Raithan said. "She looks out for me. We are hoping to procure an invitation to watch."

"Ah," the woman said. "A pity. But perhaps I can still..."

The old-fashioned door swung open, and as Eddie looked in that direction, she completely blanked out on the rest of what Chynna was saying. The person entering was human. Or mostly human.

"Sorry, I have to use the restroom," Eddie said and stood up.

A couple of the bar's patrons were approaching the newcomer. They were shouting and acting like it was his birthday or something. The young man looked the same as the last time Eddie saw him apart from a collection of fresh bruises on his pretty face. Not particularly tall, but a bundle of lean muscle. He glanced up, and for a short moment, his blue eyes looked straight at Eddie. Then he said something to one of the others and turned on his heel, making straight for the door again.

Eddie pushed through the crowd and emerged into the street in time to see the young man turn a corner. Goddamn it. He had to know she had seen him. She started running and rounded the corner, but there was no one. Eddie kicked at a loose tile on the ground. What the hell was Kierran O'Connor doing on Wenamak and in this specific city? And why was he trying to avoid her?

Most people of our generation grew up with a plethora of readily available entertainment produced by various species across the galaxy. Perhaps each species has a preference for their own take on entertainment, but it is a fact that humans have a penchant for wendek entertainment as well. I think it is due to a mix of the familiar topics and methods of storytelling that our fellow category 3 mammals employ, the fact that they have slightly higher budgets and an innate understanding of the concept of fan-service, and that we have a fascination with the otherness that is still recognizable and comfortable.

As a result, we feel familiar with a number of aspects of wendek culture and locations, be it planetary settlements or space stations. We have seen Ferthen WenKwennenth of *Worra & Darith* fame munching Crack-Shots. We have watched Ajareth DeinnunOlmeneinth from *Roamer* walk in the footsteps of legendary heroes on Ganmak so often that the mythology of that planet feels as familiar as several human ones. And so on.

But it is important to remember that wendek entertainment does not give us the full picture. This isn't something humans in general have trouble with when it comes to shows produced by other humans. But if we mainly get our knowledge of wendek from said entertainment, it can be easy to forget that it is just that and not an accurate depiction. In other words, it is important not to glamorize wendek and wendek societies. Did you know, for instance, that Wenamak's largest city, Kwipadam, has an area where only wendek outcasts and people of other species live? Tourists never go there, and wendek media is not likely to showcase this part of the city where certain wendek seek to exploit other species.

— Alannah Jackson, *Why Wendek Are Not Space Elves*

6
KIERRAN O'CONNOR

When Eddie Macías dropped him off at Stonehenge Station a few months back, Kierran O'Connor did not linger. The only reason he would ever go there was to interact with his employer at the time, and that was no longer relevant because Eddie's boss, Richard Hart, had collaborated with the Terran Defense Force to neutralize him.

Kierran sneered at the thought of the military involvement, giving his reflection in the mirror an expression that he would never allow in public. He prodded his cheekbone with his organic index finger. The swelling and angry bruising was nearly gone. The military may be the cause of most of his problems, but at least they had also given him a few perks. It was not that Kierran did not feel any pain. But the biotech in his brain suppressed most of it. Or so he assumed. Truth be told, he had only a nebulous recollection of a time when he felt pain in the way ordinary humans did. Quick healing was a gift from the military as well. Very handy in any line of work he had ever taken on.

When he hitched a ride on the first ship that was headed away from human space, Kierran was determined to put his short career as a killer for hire behind him. He had never enjoyed it, and while it paid well, there was no reason to go on when his employer was no longer in business. He also intended to put *Colibri* Investigations behind him. His agreement with Hart had come to an end, and that was for the better. Hart knew who, or rather *what*, Kierran was, and although he did not play as dirty as Kierran's old employer, that was still a huge liability.

Once in a while over the past couple of months, Kierran's thoughts had wandered to the strange little crew. If it was true that you could take a person out of the military but not take the military out of a person, Richard Hart was the perfect example. He had rigid rules for himself and the people around him.

Kierran let out a long breath. His reflection's eyebrows drew together, tugging at the fine web of scars around his artificial eye. The irony was not lost on him. The military quite literally had not been taken out of him. But there were soldiers who did not act or look like soldiers at all, like that young agent who had somehow been entangled in the team's business. 'Somehow' being synonymous with Alannah, the most confusing of Hart's crew. Kierran had scared her. That was reasonable enough, but she had also acted like... like Kierran was a person. She had insisted on smalltalk and friendly banter.

The last member of the trio was Eddie. She was obnoxious and annoying and had disliked Kierran from the beginning, which was a lot easier to handle than Alannah's strange friendliness. But now she was on Wenamak. She was in Kwipadam. It probably had nothing to do with him. Probably.

Kierran exhaled noisily. He had to compartmentalize. He had to fight tonight.

Despite his best efforts, though, Kierran was almost distracted in the ring. He could not help looking for Eddie or Richard Hart in the crowd. Being on edge like this was a very odd and not at all pleasant thing to be, so after his fights were done, Kierran decided to investigate. He could not shake the feeling that Richard Hart and his people may be in Kwipadam because of him, even if it sounded more like paranoia than a reasonable concern even to himself. Why would they come all this way for him? And, more importantly, how would they even have tracked him down? He was careful. Went through one disposable patch after another. Got lifts on spaceships whose crews didn't mind an extra passenger who paid in slightly unconventional ways, such as helping out with moving cargo. Hart couldn't possibly have tracked him to Wenamak. He had most likely come here for another purpose entirely.

But still. All Kierran had was Hart's word that he wouldn't turn him in to the Terran Defense Force, and words were broken more easily than a zetoi's bones. They might not have come here for him, but that didn't mean they wouldn't try something once they discovered him. Maybe they were in a tight spot financially and were counting on the authorities compensating them for capturing Kierran. Or that intelligence agent Alannah had befriended hadn't been as oblivious as he appeared. He might have tipped off his commanding officer who had then somehow tracked Kierran down and sent Hart after him.

There were other possibilities. Lots of them. Eddie might have quit her job and come to Wenamak on her own. Or she might be visiting the beautiful wendek guy she was talking to when Kierran spotted her.

He should forget the not-even-an-encounter. Go on as he had for these past couple of months. Or take a break from fighting and lay low for a while. He could afford that much with the earnings from the ring by now. Or he could leave. Leave Kwipadam and maybe even Wenamak behind and start over again somewhere else. He did not want to have to start over. He did not want to run again, not right now. So he decided to have a chat with Karsteth, colloquially called The Spy because she always knew what was going on in Kwipadam's underworld. She would know if *Colibri* Investigations were doing anything that could affect Kierran. Not because she cared about him, but because she cared about the gang and made sure trouble didn't find its way to its affairs.

And so it was that Kierran found himself approaching Karsteth late that night. "Kierran, my favorite human!" came the greeting when he entered the manager's office in the hotel that, if Kierran wasn't mistaken, was the location of quite a few seedy operations. She was sitting at her desk, her dark blue suit glittering in the light of the compact lamp-slash-censer in front of her. She swiped a display out of existence with one long-fingered and elegant hand as soon as Kierran was close enough to be able to make out anything on it. Her skin was paler grey than most wendek Kierran knew and made her dark brown eyes seem even larger than the average of her species. She smiled at him.

Kierran gave her a nod and then, remembering he was actually here to talk, said, "Hi." He didn't add that she probably called every human she met her favorite, but the thought did cross his mind. Although he was pretty popular in these circles, if for no other reason than his ability to efficiently beat people of any species senseless.

"Drag up a chair. What can I do for you, kid?"

Kierran preferred to stand, but he obeyed. "I am looking for information."

"Oh?" Karsteth said, her lips twisting into an even broader smile. "Well, you have come to the right person, then, haven't you? I am practically a crawler bug watching its web. What kind of information?"

Kierran appreciated how quickly she got to the heart of the matter. "I am wondering if you have any information about a couple of humans..." He trailed off.

"I am going to need a bit more than that, kid," she laughed. "Names, stills, descriptions, you know."

Kierran hesitated, though he could not say why. So what if he gave away their names? He did not owe them secrecy. "One is a woman in her mid 30s. Light brown skin, slender, a little taller than me, short, dark brown hair with a sidecut. I am positive she is in Kwipadam. The other person is male, in his mid or late 40s. Pale skin, short, black hair with greying temples. Most likely a stubble. Around 190 cm tall, of medium build and muscular."

Karsteth looked thoughtful. "And is this man handsome?"

"Yes," Kierran confirmed.

"Is he your ex-boyfriend?" she asked.

"No," Kierran said. "Why?"

She grinned at him. "Just checking. I don't want to waste my time looking into your man and his new girlfriend."

"I have not been sexually or romantically involved with either of them. Neither do I have any desire to," Kierran said to avoid any more questions along those lines. "They are known to work and travel together, which is why I think he is here too. I saw the woman last night in a bar in the mixed species area."

Karsteth shook her head slowly, signaling puzzlement. "Why are those two so important to you?"

"They are not important to me," Kierran said, more out of habit than anything else.

"And yet, here you are," Karsteth said with an broad gesture, "asking for my valuable time looking into them."

Kierran let out a long breath. "They are investigators. I had some issues with them a while back. Not on Wenamak. Before I came here. I want to make sure they are not here to cause any trouble for me."

Karsteth's expression changed. She was doing the math and, from the look of it and the change in her pheromones that Kierran's enhancements picked up on, she was reaching the conclusion that perhaps she ought to be wary of the two humans as well. "I see. All right, kid. I'll ask around and see if anything comes up. As for the payment..." She sized him up with her gaze.

Of course there was going to be payment.

"How do you feel about waiting on people in a skimpy outfit?"

Kierran schooled his expression. "What?"

"I have a friend with... shall we say alien tastes? He's hosting a party tomorrow night and I know he would appreciate someone like you handing out drinks wearing a sexy syraxh boy outfit," she explained.

"I'm afraid I have other plans," Kierran said. It was that or, 'I do not want to wear a sexy syraxh boy outfit,' and he really did not want to have to say that out loud. "Do you take units?"

"What a pity," she said. "Transfer 1500 units to me, then."

Kierran brought up his patch. "Consider it done."

[Connection established. Kellieth has entered the chat. Raithan has accepted the chat request.]

Raithan: Yes?

Kellieth: Just checking up on you, sir.

Raithan: I'm not a salek flower, Kellieth.

Kellieth: I know. But I wish you'd let me or Beth accompany you instead of working this case alone.

Raithan: You know why I don't want to be seen with you.

Kellieth: Wow. Thank you.

Raithan: You know what I mean. Besides, I'm hardly alone. Tonight I drank daazac and kissed a draever.

Kellieth: What? Did you like it?

Raithan: Well, you know what they say about draever tongues.

Kellieth: I meant the daazac.

Raithan: Who actually likes daazac?

Kellieth: Good point. Are the humans doing their part? What about the pheromone blockers?

Raithan: The humans are doing exactly what I need, and you've done an excellent job with the blockers.

Kellieth: Good. And the pilot thing?

Raithan: I haven't given it to her yet, but I will make sure she has it. And before you ask, I have also informed both Chrys and the others of the contingency plan.

Kellieth: I still think involving Chrys might not be a good idea.

Raithan: She was involved from the start. And I want to make absolutely sure no one discovers I'm not alone here. Was there anything else you wanted to discuss?

Kellieth: No, sir. Just be careful.
Raithan: You know me, Kellieth.
Kellieth: Exactly.
Raithan: Goodnight, Kellieth.

[Raithan has left the chat.]

— Written chat between Raithan WeinZalneinth and Kellieth ReinAraneinth

7
DEFINITELY NOT A FAN

"I don't suppose we need to go over the plan again?" Raithan asked when Eddie met him a few street corners away from their target location. It was evening, and the fancy buildings in this part of Kwipadam were reflecting the last rays of the local star's light, bathing the street in rainbow hues.

"Thank you," Eddie replied with an exaggerated sigh.

"For what?" Raithan asked.

"Richard always goes over the plan just one too many times. Like I'm stupid and need to be reminded."

Raithan smiled. "Have you considered that he might be the person in need of going over the plan multiple times?"

"Huh." Eddie chewed her lip. "Good point. I'll think of him as the stupid one, then. Thanks."

"That wasn't quite what I meant," Raithan said, but he didn't elaborate. "Before we go, I have something for you."

"Yeah? What's that?" Eddie asked.

Raithan reached into his fancy jacket and retrieved a small, transparent bag containing a syringe and vial that looked achingly familiar.

"Is that— Where did you get that?"

"Not important," Raithan said. He held it out to Eddie as if he was offering her a Crack-Shot or some other inconspicuous snack. "I don't expect to run into trouble, but I want you to have this as a last resort in case of complications. You can give it back to me later if you wish."

Eddie's fingers twitched as she tried to decide whether to accept or not. Richard was strict with hyper. He would never let her run around with a vial in her pocket. The doses were stored in the *Colibri's* cockpit and were only allowed for their intended use. She had been tempted almost beyond reason during dry spells when no jobs had required them to fly for a while, but she knew Richard counted, and she knew he was serious about the rules for her hyper use. And she very much wanted not to go down that road again. But this wasn't Richard's hyper. And she wasn't buying it illegally. Still... "I can't take this," she told Raithan.

He carelessly tossed the bag into the air and caught it again. "I see," he said. "You can't resist taking the dose the moment you are alone."

"I can!" Eddie said with what was meant to be a chuckle, but it didn't come out right.

"I'm sure we can find another solution if we run into trouble," the wendek said, toying with the bag. "But if you're afraid Richard will find out, you can give it back to me later and he will never know. And if you do end up needing it... Well, then that should outweigh the counter arguments. Anyway, it's your call. I'm not going to push you. If you're afraid, I'll keep it."

"I'm not afraid. But wouldn't I run into trouble with security?" Eddie asked.

"Not likely. You are a human spaceship pilot, and you can prove it. There is no reason you shouldn't have it on you," Raithan said.

"And yet, you know I don't already," Eddie commented.

"Yes, but only because I investigated your group before hiring you," Raithan replied.

"Okay. For an emergency. And if all goes well, I'll give it back to you later." Eddie took the sealed bag. She would hang on to it and prove to herself and Raithan that she could easily give it up after the mission was over.

"I will see you inside, then," Raithan said.

"Yeah. Good luck." Eddie began to make her way toward the location. The plan was simple. They each had a component of the descrambler. Once they were in, they would meet up. Eddie would give Raithan her part, and he would do the rest.

Getting in proved easy enough. Sure, the staff assumed she was there to fight, but having a spectator invitation did the trick, as Raithan had promised it would.

They checked for concealed weapons and found the syringe and the vial, and Eddie pushed up her sleeve to show the connector as she explained that human pilots often carried them. The staff accepted this and never even considered her belt buckle, and it suddenly occurred to Eddie that Raithan might have given her the little package as a decoy, that sly bastard.

The staff allowed her access to unmarked doors that led to parts of the hotel where no regular guests would go. This was the gang's base of operations, and while she and Raithan were doing their job, Richard and Alannah would be doing theirs in another part of the hotel. Eddie would wager the weapon business was probably taking place on the basement level, too.

Eddie emerged into an enormous space under the hotel. The floor sloped down toward a fighting ring in the middle. A huge screen above it showcased what was going on in the ring, which was not very much at the moment. Someone, a draever, was telling jokes in Standard, but no one paid her much attention. There was something strange about a draever comedian. Sure, draevere could crack a joke like any other species, but their tall and broad reptilian forms seemed a bit too intimidating to do standup, at least to the human eye.

Eddie wrinkled her nose. Compared to the carefully curated smells of the hotel above, the air here was saturated with alcohol, sweat and a mix of expensive wendek perfumes. The audience, all of them wendek as far as Eddie could tell, were wearing masks or nose plugs.

She slowly walked down the aisle between the benches to the bar because that was where she and Raithan had agreed to meet up. They had correctly assumed there would be one. Eddie passed a group of young wendek who were intoxicated and loud. Two of them had their facemasks off, and the others were cheering them on. Apparently it was a contest to see who could stand the alien stench the longest. As Eddie was turning away from them, one of the contestants was making retching noises. Charming.

"A drink to calm your nerves before you fight?" the person behind the bar asked Eddie. Being a draever, he towered over her.

"I'm not fighting," Eddie told them.

The draever sized her up. "Really? Why are you here, then?"

"I'm with a friend," Eddie replied and scanned the area, finally spotting Raithan. He was sauntering toward the bar, not wearing a facemask and looking completely unbothered by the smells. Which was an interesting contrast to last night when less poignant odors had made him react.

"That's your friend?" the bartender asked dubiously.

"Yep," Eddie said.

"When you say friend, do you mean sponsor or..?"

"I mean friend," Eddie said with emphasis. Was it so hard to believe she had a friend who was gorgeous even by wendek standards? For fuck's sake, she had wendek family. Alannah had a bunch of wendek friends on Tewamak. Interspecies' friendships were not rare.

"Ah, there you are," Raithan said. "Do you want a drink before we find a seat? My treat."

"Sure," Eddie said. "I'll take a beer, human style, if you have it."

"And your *friend*?" the draever asked. If his species were of the eyebrow-inclined kind, Eddie was sure he would have waggled them.

"Human beer does sound exciting," Raithan said in a way that suggested he might want to make out with it.

"Two human beers coming up," the bartender said.

"Friends can pay for each other," Eddie said as she took the cans and Raithan made the transfer on his patch.

"He thought we are a couple?" Raithan asked.

"Something like that," Eddie scoffed. "Ridiculous."

"Why?" Raithan said. "I'm not against interspecies relationships."

Most wendek were. They were especially against relationships that could result in mixed species offspring, and since humans and wendek actually were able to procreate, that meant they were considered off limits. Eddie's brother in law was pretty unpopular with his family because of that. At least they treated his kid well enough since it wasn't really his fault. "Okay," Eddie said. "But you're not my type."

Raithan's amusement grew into surprise. As if it was unimaginable that any human would find him resistible.

"You aren't wearing a mask," Eddie changed the subject, "or plugs. Aren't you kind of about to throw up or something?"

Raithan indicated a couple of free seats in one of the top rows. "There's a way around that."

"Really?" Eddie had not been aware of that. "How—"

"It's not important," Raithan brushed off the question. Okay then.

They sat down, and in the bustling to arrange themselves, Eddie unfastened her belt buckle and handed it to Raithan. He took it without a word and bent down as if to adjust the hem of his pants.

"All set," he reported as he straightened up again and took the beer Eddie was holding for him.

And at that moment, the lights in the room dimmed, and the crowd began to cheer and holler.

"Here we go," Raithan breathed. He was doing something with his patch now, probably getting ready to take stills or record.

"Welcome back! The rules of the game are simple," the wendek referee shouted, "two opponents meet in the ring. Contestants can give up and walk away at any time. Weapons are not allowed, body modifications are. The last one standing is the victor and goes on to meet their next opponent!"

Eddie took a mouthful of her drink. She wasn't a huge fan of watching desperate people beating each other up. Martial arts she could appreciate, but this... Her mind snapped to attention when the two first contestants were introduced. "Holy fuck!" she exclaimed.

Raithan's hand went to a gun holster he wasn't wearing. "What?"

"That guy," Eddie said, indicating the ring.

One of the fighters was zetoi. Eddie hadn't expected to see one here, but probably not all zetoi were too high and mighty for this kind of thing. She was even more taken aback to see the other contestant, though.

"Do you know him?" Raithan asked.

"I— sort of. Remember that guy I thought I caught a glimpse of the other night?"

"Ah," Raithan said. "Interesting. I didn't think they set people up cross-species here."

Eddie hadn't expected that, either, but then again, it would be highly unfair to set up Kierran O'Connor with a random human amateur fighter.

She could hear the audience chanting Kierran's name, which was super weird. He must be a regular. And a favorite. Eddie had seen him in action twice. Once beating the shit out of Richard, and once darting a couple of people to save her ass. He looked different now. Not any less focused or any more charming, but he wore a tight tanktop for starters. This was significant because Eddie had never seen his prosthetic arm before; only the hand, and not because he wished to show it to her. But here he was, openly showing off the mechanical parts. Most people opted for prosthetics that looked natural. Some turned theirs into a piece of art. Kierran's arm and hand were dark metal, scoffed in places as if he had ground them against a rough road. They were proportionally a good match for his muscular physique. But his artificial parts were military grade, stronger and more durable than their flesh and bone counterparts. They were also illegal. Kierran used to be an enhanced soldier, but the program had been scrapped, and he should, according to Richard, have been dismantled, whatever that meant.

The fight had begun now, and the zetoi immediately went for Kierran's face, probably meaning to claw at his eyes or something. He made a backflip that made Eddie's mind go blank. Not that she hadn't thought him capable of acrobatics. But she had never in her wildest imagination expected anything so showy from him.

The zetoi leapt, beat their wings, and swooped onto Kierran, but he flipped them around midair and landed on his feet a fraction of a second after the zetoi had landed on their back.

"Your friend is good," Raithan leaned in to tell Eddie.

"Yeah," she said, fascinated despite herself.

In another minute, the zetoi gave up and limped out of the ring, clutching their right wing.

Applause. Hollering. In the ring, Kierran accepted the attention with a wave of his hand and an expression that looked a bit like a smile. He was no great showman, that much was certain. Still, compared to what Eddie had seen of him before, this was positively extrovert behavior.

Next up was a draever who put up more of a struggle, but Kierran still was the superior fighter.

"Your friend is *very* good," Raithan corrected himself. He looked suspicious now.

Eddie leaned close to him. "Are you recording all that?" she asked.

"Mm. Why?" he replied and put his arm around her shoulder which was kind of creepy. "My apologies for making you uncomfortable," he muttered. The pheromone blocker would keep him from smelling it, but human body language wasn't that different from a wendek's. "But I would rather look like I'm hitting on you than conspiring with you."

Eddie swallowed a comment about dragging his wendek ass into the ring and kicking it if he tried to kiss her or touched anything more personal than her shoulder. But he didn't.

Eddie owed Kierran nothing. Not keeping his secret, and certainly not anything else. What if he complicated matters here, though? Eddie didn't think he had noticed her, but if he did, he might somehow end up drawing attention not only to Eddie herself, but to Alannah and Richard too because they ought to be doing some shady dealings right about now. Still, Kierran wasn't the type to make a scene. But she and Raithan were here to shut down this whole thing, and Raithan was recording him fighting. "I need to talk to him," she decided.

"Why?" Raithan asked.

Eddie shook her head as if to deny what she was about to say and do. But Alannah would be furious. For some reason, she appeared to have taken a liking to the little weirdo. And he had saved Eddie that one time. Dammit. Why did she have to be so conscientious? Anyway, she probably wouldn't have insisted under normal circumstance. But if the peace corps on Wenamak learned that an enhanced human soldier was running around beating up people for fun like this, it would not only be Kierran in trouble. It would be humanity. Probably nothing more than a slap on the wrist. It wasn't going to start a war or anything. But Richard would be super upset. He was very protective of humanity's reputation. "I need to warn him. Don't worry, I won't tell him the specifics. I'll hint that maybe he should stay away from this place for a while."

"That is not part of the plan," Raithan told her with a smile that fooled just about no one. "I have what we came for. Now we simply enjoy the show without drawing any attention to ourselves."

"I'll be super smooth," Eddie reassured him and patted his hand before pulling away from him.

A roar went up from the crowd. Kierran was fighting another draever now, and she had managed to land a blow, splitting Kierran's lip. On the huge screen, a closeup showed him wiping blood off his mouth with the back of his hand. The draever was grinning. Eddie found herself wishing she would knock him out already. Not because she wanted to see Kierran being beaten up, but she could get to him more easily if he wasn't in the ring.

That didn't happen, though. Kierran and the draever were locked in a complicated dance, but eventually, it was Kierran who got the better of her. Impressive. It was his fourth fight, and by now he was breathing hard, bleeding, and looking like someone who very much needed to sit down.

And then the referee stepped forward, neatly avoiding the blood on the floor, to announce it was time for a break and that everybody should remember to get more drinks and vapors and place some bets. Eddie stood up. "Hold my beer."

"Eddie!" Raithan said.

"I just need a word with him. I promise," she said, shoving her drink into his hand. She was on her way before he could make more objections. Maybe it wasn't proper behavior to someone who was technically her client. But Raithan wasn't her boss.

She jogged around the ring in the direction she had seen Kierran go.

"Hey," said a guard who was the closest thing to a burly wendek Eddie had ever seen. "Where you think you are going?" His Standard wasn't impressive, but it got the point across.

"I'm a friend of one of the fighters," Eddie told him. "I'd like to see him."

The guard leaned his head back, exhaling while keeping his eyes on her. "Yeah? And who is that?"

"The human who was in the ring a moment ago. Kierran," she said.

"Kierran has friends?" the guard said.

"Yeah, well, as hard as that might be to believe, here I am." Eddie shrugged. It was a harmless lie anyway.

"Usually only fans want to see him."

"Kierran has fans?" Eddie said before she could clamp her mouth shut on her surprise. "Anyway, I just want to see him and wish him good luck."

"Sorry. Spectators not allowed backstage. Only fighters."

Eddie crossed her arms over her chest.

"But," the big wendek said with a slow smile forming on his handsome face, "if you want to fight, that is fine."

She was in a hurry, and she couldn't be assed to stand here arguing with a guard. "Okay. Sure. Fine," she said. She'd wriggle her way out of that later somehow.

"You think you can give the audience a show?" he asked.

"Yeah. My middle name is showtime," Eddie said.

"You have a first name too?"

She considered using an alias, but it wasn't like anyone knew her here. "It's Eddie."

"Then it's a deal, Eddie Showtime." The guard grinned at her, then stepped aside to let her through the door.

Hey kiddo,

Yeah, Stonehenge is pretty quiet. Colonel Dietrich is keeping us on our toes, though. Last week, we did an exercise where half of us played bad guys and the others had to stop us from taking over the station. Next time we'll switch it around, which means I will be in command and have to neutralize Dietrich's coup. Don't tell anyone I said this, but I am kind of looking forward to trying.

Anyway. Sure, I can give you a rundown of real firearms. I don't know how much of it is relevant to your upcoming stream, so tell me if you need me to go more in depth with something.

We're looking at three basic types of firearms:

Kinetic guns, which rely on the kinetic impact of their projectiles (bullets) to inflict damage. I know you see them a lot in the games you play, but they are pretty much illegal in reality. Only the military/law enforcement have access to them. They still exist because they have an edge over other types when it comes to speed, range and penetration. Which is also the reason they should not be taken lightly or used by anyone who is not authorized to have them.

Next up we have dart guns which shoot out tiny darts that release a fast-working paralyzing agent when they hit their target. The exact effect depends on the type of dart ranged from A to E class with A being lethal and E causing something like intoxication. You don't necessarily get one license to own them all when you get a dart gun license. Your sister, of course, does have the whole set, but there is rarely any reason to go above C darts. I don't know anyone in the Force who has ever used a dart gun to kill another person.

Shockers are strictly speaking not in the same category as everything else on my list because they aren't ranged weapons. As you know, (remember you need to get your own permit renewed soon btw!) they are used for self-defense to shock someone with electricity. And to answer your question: No, a lethal version does not legally exist.

Finally we have EMP guns which work a lot like shockers, but without any physical contact. Like dart guns, they are normally used to temporarily stun a target, but unlike dart guns, they can have a wider area of effect and do more damage (not only to living beings, but also to electronic equipment), which is why there are more restrictions on them than on shockers.

I know you only asked about firearms, but I can't help noticing that your avatar uses a sword in some of your games. Maybe you should be looking into contemporary equivalents too? Usually sword fighting is considered a sport or a hobby, but certain soldiers actually specialize in blades even today. It's not on the normal curriculum, so they have to take special training. Usually we aren't talking claymores or svaelonger here, but I've known one soldier who used a katana, and I've had the privilege of seeing my own commanding officer train with a tactical gladius.

— Excerpt from dispatch from Captain Zaida Najjar to professional game streamer Amir Najjar

8
ACCORDING TO PLAN

The location was more or less exactly what Richard had expected of the illegal transaction. A respectable hotel sat comfortably on the edge of one of the richest neighborhoods in the city, straddling the invisible border between the fancy-holiday-still-ready part and the less savory alleys of the poor multi-species area where Chrys' clinic was located and Raithan had taken Eddie to a bar the other day.

The hotel's management were oblivious enablers at best and accomplices at worst, and Richard's units were on the second option. They could not possibly overlook both the underground fighting ring and meetings like the one he and Alannah were about to attend. The entire hotel might even be owned by the gang leader.

A guard escorted Alannah and Richard through the foyer and through a nondescript corridor, which was a rather suspicious thing in a high-end wendek location. Richard glanced down at Alannah. She was looking all right. He would really have preferred to do this on his own, but after Lejja's insistence that he brought her along, Richard felt it would seem suspicious not to. And Alannah had reassured him she was absolutely fine with continuing to play her part. Besides, it should be safe and simple enough.

The door at the end of the corridor opened when they approached, and the guard motioned for them to go through and down a flight of narrow stairs. They had already been frisked for concealed weapons. Richard was glad he wasn't the kind of person who felt nervous without a gun on him, though he had to admit he would have liked to keep a shocker in his boot.

"Ah, Richard and Alannah!" Lejja called out as they entered the room at the end of the stairwell. Though, room was a bit of an understatement. It was more like a warehouse, a labyrinthine space full of crates and boxes. This last part, Richard wasn't very happy with. He preferred being able to clearly see what was going on around him, but some of these stacks were so tall that not even a wendek would be able to look over them. There were labels on most of the crates that Alannah could read and Richard could not, but he had a feeling they were going to be inconspicuous enough and not what they were here for.

Lejja was smiling at them. He had brought two of the people from the restaurant. There was a fourth person present too, and Richard assumed he was the boss. If he had met him anywhere else, he would have guessed he was a middle manager in a company selling patch security or something similar. He was tall and wore a no-nonsense business suit and a stony expression. Of the four wendek, two were visibly armed, but Richard would bet the rest had a discreet gun tucked into a pocket or waistband.

"So glad you could make it!" Lejja continued. "This is my boss, Gerthiel. Boss, this is Richard Hart and Alannah Jackson." He stepped back to let Gerthiel take the spotlight.

"Pleased to make your acquaintance," Richard said. If he was not mistaken, Gerthiel was a Menal name, but he would have to ask Alannah for verification of that.

Next to him, Alannah said something, a greeting, probably.

"Likewise," Gerthiel said, clipped and precise. His body language did not exactly radiate pleasure. He looked at the guard behind Richard and Alannah and acknowledged something she said with two raised fingers. From the sound of it, she left the room again, and the door closed.

"Come on," Gerthiel continued and led them through a corridor of boxes to an open space with a row of unmarked crates on the floor. Now, this was what they were here for.

All they had to do now was to inspect the goods and agree on a price, a time and a location for the transaction itself, and then Raithan would take it from there. Richard assumed he would use the evidence and testimonies provided by the whole team to call in backup for the big operation in time. That was how he would have played it.

"First off," Gerthiel said, gesturing for one of his people to punch in a code on the lock of the crate and pry off the lid, "we have a nice selection of kinetic firearms."

"Hm," Richard said, not too enthusiastically, "will these come with projectiles? I need them to be anonymous, if you catch my meaning."

"Of course, of course," Gerthiel said. "We have all the ammunition you could possibly want. Bulk discounts will apply."

"Very good," Richard said. "And for something less messy?"

At his signal, Gerthiel's hench person put the lid back on, and the crate locked itself automatically. She opened one adjacent to it, and Gerthiel picked up what was unmistakably an EMP gun, although Richard did not recognize the model.

"Have you seen a gun like this before?" Gerthiel asked Alannah. Damn. She wouldn't know whether this was a common model that Richard had neglected to tell her about when he gave her a crash course before this meeting. He turned to see her reply properly.

"Have I seen a bad boy like that before?" Alannah replied and laughed. Then she smirked. "Why don't you tell me about its specs, hm?"

Richard chuckled to hide his relief that she was playing along so well.

"I would be delighted to," Gerthiel said, stroking the gun in a way that never seemed entirely healthy to Richard when people did it. "It has a range of up to 15 meters, and its built-in power supply gives it —" He stopped abruptly at the sound of the door and then rapidly approaching footsteps.

A pale wendek Richard didn't recognize appeared and made her way to Gerthiel. She side-eyed Richard and Alannah in a way Richard did not like one bit.

"What is it, Karsteth?" Gerthiel asked.

The newcomer leaned in close and said something to her boss.

Next to Richard, Alannah stiffened, and he very much wanted to ask her what was going on. But they had to play it cool.

Gerthiel threw his head back in dismay. "Lejja," she said, "we need to talk about your judgment."

"What?" Lejja asked, looking as confused as Richard felt.

"Something the matter?" Richard asked.

Gerthiel motioned for his hench people to get closer. The armed pair brought up their weapons.

Alannah gasped, and Richard really wanted to tell her it was going to be okay, but... "What the hell is going on here?" he said instead. "I don't appreciate your change of attitude. If you want to make a deal, you should really consider that."

Gerthiel took a step closer to them. "I just had a bit of new information," he said. "And I don't appreciate what I hear, Captain Richard Hart of the Terran Defense Force."

It didn't surprise Richard in the least that someone had discovered he was a former military officer. He and Raithan both assumed the gang would look into his past. "Former captain," he said. "I'm retired. What seems to be the problem?"

"Retired," Gerthiel echoed. "So we are supposed to believe an officer retired from the military at your age?"

"We aren't draevere," Richard said flatly. "It's perfectly acceptable for humans to retire. But it was a medical discharge, if you must know."

Gerthiel gave him an exaggerated once-over. "You seem in perfect health to me."

"Oi!" Alannah cut in. "You can't assume that all disabilities are visible! People shouldn't have to justify themselves to you or prove that they are struggling!"

"Thank you, Alannah," Richard said softly. As much as he genuinely did appreciate her fervor and righteousness, the timing was not great.

"I told you that from the beginning, boss" Lejja said. "And besides, they smell honest enough. I mean, they smell human, but..."

"Have you never heard of pheromone blockers?" Gerthiel's nostrils twitched in irritation. "And I know that's what the publicly available documents say." He focused on Richard again. "But it sounds like a bogus virus to me. You are an intelligence officer. Who sent you here?"

Richard put a hand on Alannah's shoulder to make sure she didn't continue the argument. "No one sent me. Why are you bringing all this up now? You had plenty of time to research us both before now. You could easily have backed out if you didn't like what you saw."

"I had some new intel. Someone warned us about you," Gerthiel said.

Warned them? Who could that possibly be? Could Raithan have double-crossed them somehow? But there was absolutely nothing he would gain from it.

"We are here to make a deal and arm a group of people, that is all," Richard said. "If you are going to waste our time with your unfounded accusations, we might as well call off this whole thing."

"Oh, I don't think you two get to walk out of here," Gerthiel said.

The two armed wendek had been moving around Richard and Alannah to stand behind them. And now Gerthiel slowly raised the EMP gun. Richard was not going to be able to talk his way out of this. He had to protect Alannah. He had to get both of them out of here. And there was no time to form a proper plan.

Lejja moved to the wall and smashed a panel with his fist. An alarm immediately screamed at them so loudly that everybody in the room flinched.

"Turn that damn thing off!" Gerthiel bellowed at him. "We don't need backup for two puny humans!"

As Lejja banged his fist against the panel again and they were all plunged into silence, Richard spun, grabbed Alannah around the waist and dragged her down with him as he dove behind a stack of crates. "Stay down!" he told her.

The closest armed wendek followed, and Richard knew he would only get this one chance to improve the odds even a little bit. He lunged at them.

There are several ways for wendek to circumvent being overwhelmed by the smells of other species, nose plugs and facemasks being the most widely known and most frequently used. However, there is a third option that is occasionally employed when the others are not viable. To put it simply, it is possible to use a special vapor drug that is breathed in through the nose. The drug consists of a concentration of non-wendek pheromones that overwhelms the imbiber's sense of smell to such an extent that it temporarily short circuits. In effect, the wendek will be numb to most smells that they may come across with the exception of certain familiar ones.

This method is highly unpleasant, though. You might compare it to getting a punch in the face instead of setting an alarm clock to wake you up. This is one of the reasons you are not likely to meet anyone who uses it. Exaggerated use can also be hazardous to a person's health, and the drug is not available without a prescription.

— Alannah Jackson, Why Wendek Are Not Space Elves

9
BORN READY

Eddie found herself in a locker room with benches and a smell like feet and blood. A couple of draevere were talking in one corner. They only spared her a brief glance. One of them had green skin and was tall and broad even for a draever. The other was brown skinned, short and streamlined in comparison, which still made him a good bit taller and bulkier than Eddie.

Kierran was sitting alone on a bench with his back against the wall, holding a bloody rag to his mouth. His eyes widened when he saw Eddie, and he sprang to his feet, ready to strangle her with the rag or punch her in the face, and Eddie wondered why she bothered.

"Stand the fuck down," she said in Standard, "I'm just here to talk!"

Kierran searched her face, and appeared to reach some conclusion in her favor. "Well?" he said in English, probably not wanting the two draevere to understand the conversation, which was fine by Eddie. "What about?"

"So when you hinted at another career path after we did you-know-what you-know-where, this is what you meant?" Eddie asked. "I suppose it's better than—"

"Get to the point," Kierran said. "What are you here for?"

"You know, if you hadn't disappeared on me in that bar, we might have talked over a beer or something," Eddie continued. He did not look amused or apologetic or anything really. A Kierran classic.

Eddie shot a glance at the other people in the room. The draevere were still deep in conversation. "I'm here to warn you, okay?" she said, her voice dropping to almost a whisper.

Kierran waited for her to go on. He didn't look particularly scared. Impressively, his lip had already stopped bleeding. A normal person would have needed stitches or at least wound sealant, but his body mended minor injuries like this on its own. She had seen it magic away a broken nose as well.

"You need to stay away from this place and lay low for a while," she said. "Someone is shutting it down."

"You and Hart?" Kierran asked.

"Not exactly. Just take my word for it. And if you are involved in anything else then you need to stop that too," she said. She really hoped he wasn't. She wanted to say that selling weapons wasn't Kierran O'Connor's style, but what did she know?

"Why are you telling me this?" he asked.

Eddie groaned. "Thank you, Eddie. It's so nice of you to tell me. I really appreciate it. Your hair looks great," she said in an imitation of his subtle Irish accent that sounded horrendous even to herself.

Kierran's gaze flicked to the top of her head. "Your hair has not changed," he said.

"Yeah well, neither have you!" she retorted. "I'm telling you because it's what Alannah would do and because it would look bad if anyone found out about you and shipped you back to the Terran Defense Force, okay?"

Kierran's jaw clenched and unclenched. "All right. I— thank you."

"That's better."

"Kierran, you ready?" It was the huge wendek from outside poking his head in.

Kierran tossed the rag aside. "Yes," he said.

"Yaan, can we put that human in before you?" the guard asked, meaning Eddie.

The shorter of the draevere, Yaan, studied Eddie. "Um, sure," he said, looking a bit taken aback. "But she knows, right? She's seen him fight, I mean?"

"Actually, I changed my mind," Eddie said before anyone could reply. "I don't think I'm going to fight anyway. Sorry for the trouble."

"No," the guard said, "you can't talk your way out of it. You said you fight, you fight. That's the rule."

"But I... slammed my knee into one of the benches and it really hurts," Eddie said, reaching down to massage her left knee with a wince that she hoped looked genuine.

"That's not how it works," the guard said.

Kierran cleared his throat. "Fight me for a few seconds," he said in English. "Pretend I knock you out right away. No one will suspect anything."

Eddie turned on him. "Oh, that's how it is? You're so amazing and you want me to look like an idiot trying to fight you? I'm weak, is that it?"

"Well," Kierran said, "you are compared to me."

"You know what? Let's do this. Let's do this," she repeated in Standard. "I'll teach him a lesson!"

The tall draever laughed out loud, and Yaan looked positively shocked.

"Hey!" Eddie said, pointing at them. "Don't give me that!" The thing was that Eddie's temper was probably a bit hotter than her fighting abilities. But she wasn't a pushover. She knew that for sure because she had sparred with Richard on occasion, and she had been in her fair share of fistfights. And... she had an ace up her sleeve. Literally. She took off her jacket and rolled up said sleeve. "You don't have any policies against human pilots, do you?"

The guard's head tilted back in surprise. "I don't think so, but—"

"Good. Cause if you want me to fight, I'll do this," she said. Before anyone could stop her, Eddie had slipped out the small bag from her pocket. She ripped off the seal, uncapped the vial with her teeth, filled the syringe and pushed the contents into the connector on her arm.

"Shit," the guard said. "That's hardcore. Okay, I let you do it. It's only one fight anyway. You okay with it?" The last part was aimed at Kierran.

"Yes," he said without hesitation.

"What do you mean it's only one fight? Who says I'm not going to win?" Eddie asked. She took a deep breath. The hyper was already starting to flow through her body.

"Keep telling yourself that, mammal," the tall draever said, her words slowing down from Eddie's subjective point of view even as she spoke.

Eddie turned on her. "I'll take you after I kick his ass. And his," she added, pointing first at Kierran and then at the other draever because this was what hyper did to Eddie when she wasn't in a cockpit and had somewhere to direct her energy. She got jittery and cocky and knew she was invincible. Already, people around her were moving in slow motion.

She looked at Kierran. Everything became sharper with hyper, and her senses became faster. She wondered if maybe she would actually be able to beat Kierran. She thought that probably she would. She thought that sober Eddie would be a bit more hesitant with that conclusion, but this was Eddie honed to a knife point. And she would never have caught it before, but she saw Kierran suppress a teeny tiny smirk.

"Okay, get her ready, and I tell management," the wendek said and disappeared.

"I was born ready!" Eddie called after him.

The short draever made his way to the two humans as Kierran adjusted the protective cloth strips around his hands.

"Here," Yaan said. "I'll wrap you."

"Oh. Thanks," Eddie replied.

"You're a pilot?" he asked as he began to wrap the strips around her hands and wrists in a practiced way.

"Yeah," she said.

"Draever pilots don't need drugs," he continued. This was common knowledge, and Eddie wondered where he was going with it. "But I thought you only used them when you need to go through hyperspace?"

Eddie suppressed a sigh. What the actual fuck? Was she being lectured by a random draever fighter about hyper? "I mean, that's what it's for," she said. "But it has other uses too."

Yaan looked at her face, only meeting her gaze with his yellow, slit-pupiled eyes for a brief moment. As a rule, draevere avoided too much eye contact unless they were about to beat you up or kiss you. "I meant no offense. It's none of my business," he said. "There, good to go. Don't go easy on K, all right? Seriously though, there's no shame in giving up. You don't have to let him beat you to a pulp."

Eddie tried to scoff, but it came out as a bit of a weak laugh. "Thanks," she said and then, because this guy was actually pretty nice to her and she was in a charitable mood, "Hey, Yaan, you might not want to stick around here for long."

"What?" he asked.

"It'd be better for you to find something else to do. Like, really, really soon. Trust me," she said.

Yaan didn't look like he believed her, but that was all she could do.

The wendek guard returned once more. "Okay, get out there, do your best. Fight fair," he told them.

Kierran took the lead. Noise exploded around Eddie when she followed him out of the locker room. The referee was shouting into his voice amplifier, telling everybody how amazing Kierran was, and Kierran stepped into the ring, accepting the applause.

"You have seen him fight draevere twice his size. You have seen him fight blindfolded and with his hands tied," the referee shouted.

"What?" Eddie muttered to no one in particular.

"But now, a human hyperspace pilot has challenged him! Yes, that's right! A pilot high on hyper! I introduce to you Eddie Showtime!"

She should have come up with something better. But now she was jogging into the ring, blinded by spotlights, to a cacophony of applause and shouts from the spectators, and it suddenly hit her that Raithan would kill her. And then she realized that what she really ought to be worried about was Richard finding out about this. Fuck. But here she was.

Eddie waved at the audience, then turned to Kierran.

"Eddie, don't—" he began in an undertone.

"Shut up and fight, pretty boy," Eddie told him. She raised her fists and bumped them against Kierran's like she had seen him do with his other opponents.

Then they stepped back, and Eddie forgot a probably very exasperated FWSA agent holding her beer somewhere in the sea of lights and faces. She forgot how disappointed Alannah would be if she found out, and how furious Richard would be. She wanted to kick Kierran's ass. She wanted to see how a pilot on hyper would do against an enhanced soldier. He might be superhuman, but so was she. At the moment, at least.

Kierran's face was set in concentration or, Eddie thought, maybe that was reading too much into his default humorless expression. A couple of tiny drone cameras that she had not noticed before were circling the two of them. Possibly, her face was now on the huge screen above the stage.

When the match began, Kierran hung back in a neutral, defensive stance. Waiting for her to make a move. Assassin-Kierran would strike first and with lethal precision. Prizefighter-Kierran was giving his opponent time, was probably reading their moves too. Well, Eddie wasn't here to tip-toe around him. She was here to— To take him down a notch or two, she decided. Yeah. That was it.

She feigned a punch at his face and went for his midsection instead. Kierran dodged both. But he looked surprised and adjusted his posture. Hah, finally realizing that a pilot on hyper wasn't to be trifled with.

When Kierran did attack her, Eddie danced around him and kicked at the back of his legs, sending him stumbling forward before he could catch himself.

The crowd went wild. Their voices came at Eddie in a slow wave, and the referee was hollering too. Not used to seeing a mere human touch their beloved little soldier, huh?

Kierran turned around to face her again. Now he was definitely smiling. Not a big, hearty grin or anything, but smiling nonetheless.

"Been bored here?" Eddie asked him, not sure if he could hear her over the roar on all sides of the ring.

Kierran didn't reply, and his smile disappeared quickly, but it had been there. Even if Eddie didn't win the match, she considered that a fucking big victory.

And she had barely thought that before she only narrowly escaped Kierran's metal fist. Without hyper, that would have caught her right in the face. Which, regrettably, the next jab did.

Eddie stumbled back, her own hand reflexively reaching up to touch her jaw. She did not feel the pain as acutely as she would have without hyper. But he had used his organic left hand for that, and she was pretty sure he'd held back. Which pissed her off to no end, truth be told. She flew at him and landed a foot right in his chest. He really was slow. Or slower than her. Clearly, she had the edge on him when it came to speed, but she would be an idiot to think she was the stronger of the two. Even on hyper, she wasn't that cocksure. She danced forward to follow up while he was still recovering his balance and—

And then the scream of a siren blared out so loudly that Eddie could hardly hear anything else. It cut out right away, and in the silence that followed, Eddie could just make out what sounded like rapid kinetic gunfire from somewhere.

A second later, people started screaming. Beyond the ring, there was commotion. Spectators trying to get out. Others trying to calm down everybody. But Eddie didn't care. She started toward the edge of the ring.

"Was that your doing?" Kierran asked, taking hold of her arm.

"No!" she said, jerking back. "But I have to go. Now. And you should too!"

He released her, and Eddie vaulted over the rope. Whatever had happened, she had a nasty feeling it had something to do with Richard and Alannah. It couldn't be that hard to find them, so she was damn well going to check up on the situation. Even if they weren't involved, it wouldn't hurt. Probably she should wait for Raithan, but... No. It was more simple this way.

Kierran was running at full speed, almost keeping up with her. "This is not what I meant!" she told him.

"Just do what you have to," he told her. And Eddie knew she was not going to be able to shake him off.

Pelreith: The trailer for the 12th season of *Worra & Darith* just dropped, and VoidNet is overflowing with reaction clips and speculations. It seems to me like the personal stakes are higher for our favorite investigators this time around. I am your host, Pelreith QunBoyaneinth, and I have the actors who play the dynamic duo, Najeiwa SeinnunQueneinth and Ferthen WenKwennenth, with me in the studio today. Can you two shed any light on what is going on in the trailer? I'm obviously talking about Worra's monologue.

Ferthen: It's a deep one. "If I had known the shadows from their past were creeping up on them, I would have told Darith how much I care. But we never know how much we take for granted until it is too late."

Najeiwa: I like your version of Worra.

Ferthen: Thanks!

Pelreith: So can you say anything about it?

Najeiwa: I mean, we've reached a point in the show where everyone expects the main characters to bounce back from injuries and, you know, experiences that would traumatize people in real life.

Ferthen: Careful, Najeiwa.

Najeiwa: I'm not spoiling anything! I'm just saying, the show can be... What's the word? Things happen in a certain way that you have come to expect.

Ferthen: Formulaic?

Najeiwa: Yeah, formulaic, thank you. There's nothing wrong with that, but sometimes you have to stir things up. The writers really did that with season 12. I think it will surprise a lot of viewers. And I think it brings up a lot of important topics, too. The stakes are really high in this season, and we are going to see some big changes taking place.

Pelreith: How do you think the fandom is going to react?

Najeiwa: I mean, it's a big deal when you have an established cast and people think they know the characters and then you suddenly drop a bomb on them. I think the fans will find season 12 darker, in a way, but also deeper.

Ferthen: True, true. But I think if the writing is good enough, it can work really well, and we have some excellent writers on the show. Yes, it's got action and fast, snappy dialog, but there is still room for those deeper, personal storylines if they are treated right. With respect, you know?

— Interview on VoidNet with Najeiwa SeinnunQueneinth and Ferthen WenKwennenth

10
UNBELIEVABLY IMPRESSIVE MOVES

"Stay down!" Richard told Alannah after he tackled her to the ground in a way that made Alannah feel like a bag of ripeth. A bag of, she had to amend, terrified ripeth. But right now, the emotional capacity of a root vegetable would be preferable to the way her heart hammered in her chest and her breath threatened to turn into hyperventilation.

Richard was already gone and although Alannah very much intended to follow his orders, she edged closer to the corner of the crates hiding her. From this vantage point, she saw Richard land an elbow hard in the face of the closest wendek, somehow turn around with the opponent's wrist clasped firmly and pull the gun out of their hand in a way that made Alannah's own self-defense capacities look like a joke.

There was movement behind the two of them, and Alannah spotted another wendek with a gun the instant Richard wrenched the person he was fighting around, effectively putting them in the line of fire. They twitched and crumpled to the floor.

Richard dove back down next to Alannah. She had never seen his face this concentrated before.

"Are you okay? Did you mean for that to happen?" she asked.

"We need to get out of here," Richard said. Alannah couldn't blame him for ignoring her questions or not having the presence of mind to lipread. "We can't take them all."

'We' was a bit generous, Alannah thought.

Richard held out the gun he had taken from the wendek. It was a kinetic gun. "Take it. I need you to lay down cover fire!"

"But!" she protested. Now obviously wasn't the time to talk about her dislike for weapons, and kinetic guns in particular, or her absolute horror at the thought of killing another person. But she had no idea if she could be of any use here.

"I only need you to stay hidden and shoot in their general direction. You can do that. I'm going to create a diversion—"

New voices in the room. Shouting in Synal. Oh no, that meant backup had arrived.

Richard turned to Alannah.

"The humans are hiding. One is armed," she translated Gerthiel's words. "Take them alive." Well, that was good. "Spread out and surround them."

Richard sneered. "Change of plan. There's an emergency exit that way," he told Alannah, indicating the direction with a tilt of his head. "Shoot when I tell you to. Then stay behind cover and get out if you can. Run for it, hide and contact Eddie and Raithan."

"What about you?" Alannah asked. But he wasn't looking at her.

"It's an order," he added. Which, as per their contract, meant she had to comply. She had to trust his plan.

Richard moved away from her to the other end of the crate. "Now," he said.

Alannah peeked over the top of the barrier, thankful that it was a solid construction. She fired the gun in the approximate direction where she had last heard someone talking. The recoil was not bad, but she still felt it jerk back her shoulders and arms. When she ducked back down, Richard was gone once more.

There was probably a pattern to his movements, a reason for his going after the person he did and not someone else. But all Alannah knew was that she was firing at intervals and that there was shouting in Synal and rapid gunfire all around her. There was the weird crackle of EMP weapons mingled with kinetic gun shots. And then a loud noise from somewhere behind her, and Alannah whipped around in time to see the emergency exit open so violently the door bounced on the wall.

And— Alannah barely managed to suppress a cry of relief. It was Eddie. And Kierran, which was weird, but Alannah assumed Eddie had met him somewhere and brought him to help. Eddie spotted Alannah and went straight for her. Kierran, on the other hand, scaled a pile of crates and, impossibly, leaped off them, landing more or less on top of a wendek before anyone, Alannah included although she saw him do it, could process what was going on.

"You okay?" Eddie asked.

"Yes," Alannah replied. Eddie had come to her to make sure she was all right. That was really sweet, but Richard was—

"Give me the gun," Eddie said and ripped it out of Alannah's hands. Her own were wrapped in what looked like protective cloth strips, for some reason. All right, so she hadn't only gone for Alannah to make sure she was unscathed. Alannah would not hold that against her. "Stay," Eddie added and rolled out from behind their hiding place, actually firing the weapon at the same time, which was, regardless of how little Alannah liked to admit it, unbelievably impressive.

There was a loud crack, and everything went dark. Then a reddish glow illuminated the room. A fusepanel on the wall was on fire, sparks raining down and smoke billowing from it.

"Everybody stay where you are and drop your weapons!" a new voice shouted in Synal with a familiar Menal accent and then repeated it in Standard.

Alannah turned to see Raithan in the door Eddie and Kierran had come through. Oh, that was good. With him here... She didn't even complete that thought before there was a crack, and the wendek agent was slammed into the wall by the force of a kinetic projectile. He slumped to the floor, limp and without a sound. No, no, no! Alannah had to do something. She began to crawl toward him.

The sprinklers in the ceiling finally reacted to the small bonfire created by the fusepanel. Torrents of water began to pour down.

Alannah tried to gauge where everybody was. Eddie behind a barricade of crates to the left of her, crouching and waiting to shoot again. Richard, briefly distracted by the water. At exactly that moment, Lejja popped up from his cover.

"Richard!" Alannah screamed. He wouldn't understand it, but maybe he would be startled by the sound and move.

He didn't. Alannah saw Lejja pull the trigger, saw the flash of the EMP gun, and then—

Kierran came barreling through the air, hitting Richard and toppling them both over. One of them cried out, but Alannah couldn't tell who.

"Come on, come on!" someone was yelling in Synal. "Any of you humans move, and your wendek friend gets it!"

Alannah swiveled around once more, this time to see the wendek who had tipped Lejja off about them near the door with a dazed-looking Raithan propped up against her. Alive, thankfully, and at least semi-conscious. Alannah hoped he was wearing a bulletproof vest under his shirt. Not that it would help him against the gun Karsteth was holding to his temple.

"Come on!" Karsteth screamed again. "Drop your weapons, thakking humans!"

Alannah wished she could think of some heroic trick that would save the day. But the number of people who could suddenly appear to turn the tide was used up at this point.

All the gang members ran toward Karsteth, and she waited for them to pass before backing away, still with Raithan clutched to her front.

"Alannah! Eddie!" Richard barked when the door slammed shut, and they both ran from their respective covers to him and Kierran.

"Status!" Richard said.

"All good here," Eddie said.

"I'm fine," Alannah added. "Is Kierran—"

Richard was crouched on the wet floor next to a motionless and very pale, even for him, Kierran.

"It was an EMP. I don't know if—" Richard began.

Kierran's eyes shot open, and his hands spasmed. Then his whole body convulsed.

"O'Connor!" Richard shouted, pinning him down to keep him from hurting himself. "Status, Kierran O'Connor!"

If he thought he could startle Kierran out of it, he was wrong. Kierran didn't appear to see or hear anything. As suddenly as they had begun, the convulsions stopped, leaving the him lifeless on the floor.

And that was when the sirens began, in earnest this time.

"We need to get out of here," Richard said.

"They took Raithan," Eddie said.

"Is Kierran going to be okay?" Alannah asked. "Shouldn't we wait here for the firefighters?"

Richard brushed sweat and water off his face. "We have to leave," he insisted. "We can't turn O'Connor over to the local peace corps, and we can't let ourselves be detained. Besides, Raithan had a contingency plan. We'll smash two asteroids with one demolition beam and go to Chrys' clinic."

95

A few minutes ago, we received word of a disturbance in a hotel in the center of Kwipadam. Passersby say that guests in the hotel began to pour into the street in disarray after a fire alarm went off and the sprinkler system began to douse the whole place.

"I heard gunfire somewhere in the hotel just before the fire alarms started," said one hotel guest who was drenched and clearly shaken when we talked to them.

Firefighters and the peace corps quickly arrived. According to their statements, there was a malfunction with a fusepanel in the basement, and there is nothing to worry about. More about the story as the situation develops.

— Wenamak PlaNet newscast

11
SAFETY OVERRIDE

The four humans emerged into a warm and humid Kwipadam night. It was not raining, but the sky was starless, and Richard would not have been able to find Wenamak's orbiting space station if he tried.

The only good thing about this part of the city was not a good thing at all, he thought. It was the fact that nobody batted an eye at a group of humans hurrying through the street, soaked through and one of them carrying a lifeless body.

"Come on!" Eddie urged Richard and Alannah. She was practically trotting backward trying to accelerate things, but there was a limit to how fast Richard could move while carrying O'Connor.

As focused as he was on the string of tasks ahead of him, Richard could not help noticing certain changes in his pilot. He had no idea why her hands were wrapped in protective cloth like O'Connor's, but that was not his main concern. In addition to her pace, her speech was faster, too, more clipped and impatient, and her body language had changed. The drug pilots used was not only highly addictive; it also had a lot of side effects that no one really talked about, like the shift of personality.

"Are you on hyper?" Richard asked. He wasn't sure why he did. Maybe it was to alert Alannah in case she hadn't noticed. Maybe it was to see if Eddie would lie.

"That's not important right now!" Eddie snapped.

"Where did you get it?" Alannah asked.

"Raithan gave it to me, but it's really not important right now, is it?" Eddie retorted in the kind of way she normally reserved for people she didn't particularly like.

Richard gritted his teeth. Eddie being high was not on his immediate top three of priorities, no, but why the hell had Raithan given her hyper? And why had she been stupid enough to accept it? They were going to have a conversation later. One with a capital C. "Was O'Connor in the fighting ring?" Richard changed the subject.

"Yeah. I went to warn him that it was going to get shut down," Eddie replied, biting the cuticle on one of her fingers. "And before you say anything, if I hadn't done that, he wouldn't have taken that shot for you, so I pretty much saved you!"

Richard wasn't going to address any of that right now. O'Connor had indeed taken a shot for him. One that might have killed Richard and clearly had done a lot of damage to O'Connor himself. That was one reason he wanted to get to a human doctor. The other reason was that it would look really bad if the Wenamak authorities discovered an illegal human military experiment on their planet.

He also needed to get to Chrys because she was Raithan's contingency plan. She would, hopefully, be able to contact someone who could retrieve Raithan if they could figure out where the arms dealers had taken him. And Richard couldn't help wondering if it was already too late. They had taken Raithan to keep Richard and his people from following, but did they really need him after that? Richard hoped they would keep the agent as insurance, but he also knew that if they did keep him alive, it was probably to interrogate him.

The clinic was closed for the night.

"Emergency panel," Alannah said and punched a panel next to the door.

"Is she even still there?" Eddie asked.

After an agonizing moment of waiting, during which Richard almost dropped O'Connor because the enhanced had another fit of convulsions, the door slid open. "Richard?" Chrys said. She took one look at his burden and waved him through. "What's the situation?"

"He was shot by an EMP gun. Illegal and with a powerful charge." Richard followed her through the waiting area to the examination room.

"Put him on the table," Chrys said. Richard really appreciated her efficiency and focus on the task ahead.

He carefully lowered O'Connor onto the examination table.

"When? Has he been unconscious ever since?" Chrys said, pulling on gloves and swiping at her patch to get up a medical display of some kind.

"Around 15 minutes ago. He seems to wake up at intervals and has strong convulsions. Twice since then, but he is not responsive," Richard reported.

"Does he have any implants?" Chrys asked. She was prying open O'Connor's eyelids and shining a light into his eyes. "At least an ocular one," she concluded.

Richard swallowed. "He has others too, I'm pretty sure. And a prosthetic arm if that's of any consequence."

The doctor pulled up O'Connor's shirt. Listened to his heart. Frowned.

Before Richard could ask her what was the matter, O'Connor gasped, and his body spasmed again. Richard rushed forward to keep him from falling off the table.

O'Connor's blue eyes were open, but they didn't seem to focus on anything. The fingers of his left hand gripped at nothing. His artificial right arm was limp.

"O'Connor!" Richard said, holding him still. "It's going to be fine."

Eddie and Alannah were talking, but Richard didn't have time to see what they were saying.

Chrys had turned away for a moment. Now she bent over her patient again, taking hold of his head and pressing a device to his nose. "Breathe in," she said.

O'Connor didn't appear to hear her.

"Close his mouth," Chrys said.

Alannah appeared next to Richard and did as Chrys asked, effectively forcing him to breathe through his nose.

A few seconds later, his body grew slack once more.

"That should keep him calm while I figure out what I can do for him." Chrys put the device back on the stand next to the table. "Wait outside," she added.

So Richard, Eddie and Alannah obediently filed out into the waiting area.

Richard was already making plans, arranging his possible next steps into neat groups when Alannah spoke.

"... normal reaction? Is he going to be okay?" she was asking.

"No, but the freak's got a lot of implants and stuff, right? That's probably why the EMP made such a mess of things," Eddie replied. "I'm sure he'll be okay, though. He's a tough little bastard, right?"

"Yes, to both," Richard said, leaning against the wall from a vantage point where he could see both of them talking. "Hopefully Chrys can reboot him or something." He had no idea how it worked, truth be told.

"He's not a patch!" Alannah said.

"It was pretty badass how he took that shot for you." Eddie was picking at a hole in her pant leg that Richard wasn't sure had been there earlier, or if it had ripped during the showdown.

"What would the EMP have done to you?" Alannah asked.

Richard tapped the floor with the toe of his boot. He hadn't had the time to examine that gun properly or ask questions before everything went down the black hole, but he knew what kind of equipment Gerthiel had on offer. "He might have saved my life," Richard said. He was pretty sure that was the case.

Chrys appeared in the doorway after a few minutes that had dragged on from Richard's point of view. He imagined it felt like far longer for Eddie.

The doctor looked more than a little exasperated. "Richard Hart," she said, "you have brought an enhanced soldier into my clinic!"

"Former soldier, but yes," Richard conceded. "I didn't want to risk involving anyone else, and I also need to know your—"

"How is he? Is he going to be okay?" Alannah interrupted.

"I can keep him comfortable for now. And I might be able to reboot the simple implants, but this is not my area. You need someone specific for this. A surgeon, probably, who is an expert in augmentation and biotech."

"Do you know one?" Eddie asked. "Someone who will do it off the record?"

Chrys sighed. A long, deliberate breath as if she was considering her options. "There is a person I work with sometimes. They are a neurosurgeon, and I'm sure they could do it if your soldier were wendek. Still, they can probably—" Chrys cut herself off and looked down at the patch on her wrist. "What is Raithan doing?"

"I was getting to that," Richard said. "During the incident when O'Connor was shot, Raithan was taken hostage by the—"

"What?" Chrys exclaimed, her professionally concerned expression evaporating. "You come in here asking me to help an illegal killing machine, and you neglect to tell me Raithan was abducted?"

"I honestly was getting to it," Richard said. Alannah and Eddie had both interrupted him before he could bring it up. "That's the second reason we came here. He told us that in case something unexpected happened and we can't get in touch with him, we should go to you. That there's a contingency plan."

"He might have been dead by now!" Chrys raged. "Get your priorities straight, Richard!"

Richard held up both hands to fend off the volley of words. "Chances are they figured out we work for him and took him as security and to get information from him. Find out if someone else is involved in his business, if their affiliates on other planets are in danger of investigation too. So... Do you know whom we need to get in touch with?"

Chrys looked like she wanted to slap him. Richard couldn't blame her.

"How do you know he isn't dead?" Eddie asked, indelicately.

"He just activated a tracking signal that is sent to my patch," Chrys said. "He's moving away from the city. I have his emergency contacts, but it will take them time to get here. You need to save him."

"What about the local peace corps?" Alannah asked. "Shouldn't we contact them?"

Chrys shook her head. "Raithan's investigation is very sensitive. I don't know the details, but a number of departments could be involved, and if we get the wrong one... We can't exactly ask burglary to step in here. Please, Richard. Go save Raithan." Seeing his hesitation, Chrys folded her arms over her chest. "I will get hold of my associate to help your enhanced soldier if you do."

"That's blackmail!" Eddie exclaimed.

"Technically, it's coercion," Chrys said. "I'll forward the tracking signal and Raithan's contact's details to you, Richard. Take my groundwheeler and go."

"Richard?" Alannah said.

"Fine." What choice did he really have? Even without Chrys' caveat, he would have agreed. Raithan was technically his client right now, and although saving him from abductors was not verbatim in their contract, it kind of went without saying that Richard would do his utmost in a case like this. "I'll do what I can."

"I'll drive," Eddie said, jabbing a finger in Richard's direction. "Shut up, Dick. I'm a better driver than you under normal circumstances, *and* I'm on hyper."

Chrys looked at Richard for confirmation, which he gave her with a nod. "All right. Eddie, my groundwheeler has a safety override. The code is 123456789."

"Seriously?" Eddie asked.

"Yes, I'm a doctor. Sometimes I need to get to an emergency quickly," Chrys said.

"No, yeah, I got that," Eddie snorted. "But the code!"

Richard cleared his throat.

"I can come too," Alannah said.

"Don't take it the wrong way, but I'd rather you didn't," Richard told her. "Stay here and let us know how O'Connor is doing. He'll probably be in need of a friendly face."

Said face looked more concerned than friendly right now. But Alannah dipped her chin and hugged Eddie and said something Richard didn't catch. "Be careful," she told him.

"We will," he said.

"Alannah," Eddie said as they were about to depart, "when Kierran wakes up, tell him to get better or I will kick his ass. Like I would have anyway."

There was, Richard was sure, a story there that he would have to ask about although he really rather would not.

"I will," Alannah said.

Richard's patch lit up with the tracking signal rerouted from Chrys, and he gestured for Eddie to follow him out of the clinic. But she cut in front of him and left first, of course.

Generally speaking, modern space stations are entirely safe. Artificial gravity, perfect atmospheric control, smooth public transport systems and the presence of both military and civilian security are just a few of the comforts we are used to. Should a meteor be on collision course with a space station, it is in fact a much safer place than a planet in the same situation because of the station's protective pelso plating.

However, despite the over all safety of space stations, sometimes tragic accidents do happen like in every other place. Yesterday, our home was the scene of such an accident. Despite rumors, it was not a question of terrorism, and neither were draever operatives involved. It was simply a series of extremely unfortunate malfunctions that caused a pipeline car to be derailed and fall onto another level of the station. As we have seen in both official and unofficial clips, the building it crashed into sustained massive damages, and a fire broke out. As luck would have it, the pipeline car was empty, but several people were injured in or near the collapsed building. Tragically, three citizens of Yellowstone lost their lives, and one person is still missing.

There will be a memorial tomorrow at the site of the accident at 1500 hours, local time.

— Excerpt from statement by General Wilson Nkosi, Yellowstone military security

12
NEURAL PATHWAYS

"Kierran?"

He had no idea how much time had passed, which was strange. Usually, his internal chronometer was one of many features he could consult with literally a thought. He always knew how long he had spent on any given task. Or sleeping. Or being unconscious. But right now, there was a blank.

"Kierran?" Another voice. Alannah Jackson's.

Kierran opened his eyes. He was lying on his back, and something was amiss with his sight. His right eye, the organic one, worked. It was a little difficult to focus, but he was clearly under the influence of some kind of drug. He was receiving no signals at all from his artificial eye.

Alannah was standing next to him. A little blurry and without any of the overlays Kierran was used to. He could not detect her body heat or heart rate at all. Which made sense if his left eye was out of commission.

He knew he should be more upset at his own lack of reaction to the malfunction, but all he felt was fatigue and confusion.

There was no sign of Richard Hart or Eddie nearby. Kierran felt they should be there, though at the moment, he couldn't say why. What would make him expect those two anywhere near his person? Two strangers, however, were in the room, and for one weird instant, he wondered if maybe they actually were Hart and Eddie seen without his augmented vision. But no. One was a human, a medical professional judging from her attire. The other was an oddly disheveled wendek, as if they had been woken up in the middle of the night. Was it the middle of the night?

"The sedation is wearing off now," the doctor told the others in Standard. "He'll be—"

Kierran didn't hear what she thought he would be. What felt like an electric shock went through his brain, momentarily blinding him, sharp pain jolting his whole body. He thought he heard someone cry out. It might be him.

This was wrong. Kierran O'Connor had pain suppressors. No, they did not make pain disappear because, as he had been told during training, if you did not feel pain, you grew careless and sloppy. But they usually made everything manageable, injuries inconvenient rather than debilitating. Now every part of his body was on fire. He tried to breathe, but the air didn't work properly, or else it was his lack of control of his own lungs.

"Hold him." The doctor speaking.

Hands on his shoulders. Pressure. Something over his face.

"Breathe, Kierran!"

He tried. The pain did not stop, and his body felt wrong. Heavy and uncontrollable at the same time. But his mind grew a little more clear.

The pressure on his face disappeared. Kierran was looking up into Alannah's worried face.

"Wow," the wendek said. They were scrutinizing a display floating in the air over their patch. "The numbers are all over the place."

"How do you feel?" the doctor asked.

"Fine," Kierran said.

The doctor sighed with more passion than Kierran had ever heard anyone do. "Look, I promised Richard I'd help you. Let's not waste time on urnollshit. We need as precise data as possible to fix your augmentations. Understand?"

"Yes." Kierran swallowed. His mouth was dry. The recent, from his point of view, past was coming back to him. The ridiculous fight Eddie had insisted on. The alarm. The decision to go with Eddie to see what was going on in the hotel because... He wasn't sure why. Because she had come to warn him and he did not want to be in *Colibri Investigations'* debt? Because he thought that maybe Alannah was in trouble and he could not seem to get over the notion that she had been *nice* to him once, useless and unimportant as it was? But he had followed Eddie, and Alannah and Hart had been in a mess of a situation that someone like Hart really should have been able to avoid, and Kierran had stepped in to take out their opponents, and then... And then, because he had to know if all this pain was completely in vain, "Where is Hart? And Eddie?"

"They're okay, Kierran," Alannah said. "You saved Richard's life. So just concentrate on getting better, okay?"

The doctor cleared her throat. "So, how do you feel, Kierran?"

Kierran blinked. He really could not access any information. He could not recall his augmentations ever not being there to tell him exactly where he was hurt and how bad it was. "I am unable to access any data," he said.

"We know. I want you to tell me what you are experiencing," the doctor said.

"I am experiencing," Kierran got out, "confusion. Paralyzing pain in my head at intervals. Constant pressure in my chest. I have no control of my right arm. My left eye is not working. I am experiencing occasional flashes of uncomfortable connection to both. My pain suppressors are not working."

"Do you remember what happened to you?" asked the doctor.

"I was shot by an EMP weapon."

The doctor raised her hand and tapped the air with two fingers like a wendek nod. "Jerra?"

"One moment," the wendek said, their fingers tracking something on the display.

Kierran opened his mouth to ask a question, but in that instant, pain flared through his head again and he had to focus on not screaming.

"Can't you give him more painkillers?" Alannah asked. Kierran didn't need any of the tools usually at his disposal to pick up on the worry in her voice.

"Not yet. Jerra needs to look at his data," the doctor said.

Kierran's left hand was clutching at something.

"It'll be okay," Alannah told him. She was holding his organic hand now. He wondered why. He also wondered why he didn't mind the physical contact.

"Okay, I have what I need. Let's get him prepped." The wendek, Jerra, again.

"What are you going to do?" Kierran managed.

Jerra stepped closer. "I'm a neurosurgeon. I mean, I usually work on wendek, but your brain isn't that different from ours. We have pretty much the same parts, and I, um, did take a comprehensive course on human brains." They cleared their throat and smiled in a way that was probably meant to be reassuring. It was not. "So what happened is that the EMP knocked out all of your implants and augmentations for a while," they said.

Kierran tried to focus on the words, but it was hard to comprehend anything right now.

"They are trying to come back online," Jerra continued, "but some circuits need replacing and others seem to be misfiring. I'm going to do as many repairs as I can, but I'm going to have to do a hard reset too."

"What is a hard reset?" Alannah asked, still holding Kierran's hand.

"It means I need to power everything down and then jumpstart him."

"Jerra means," the doctor cut in, "that after doing the repairs and replacements, they will reset the systems so they don't continue looking for neural pathways that aren't there anymore and connect to the new ones instead. That is done by stopping the patient's heart for a moment."

"We're essentially going to give you a heart attack," Jerra said to Kierran who did not need it spelled out. "But don't worry. You are not going to feel anything before we bring you back, and by then, everything should be working."

"Is it safe?" Alannah asked.

"I mean, relatively," Jerra replied. "I have done this before on wendek. Not with the same type of implants because these are very interesting—" They cut themself off. "I mean, these are human-made and clearly of the illegal sort. But the principles are the same. There is a small risk involved, and it's slightly higher because this isn't a facility designed for this kind of work." They looked at Kierran. "But your friend here says you don't want to go to a hospital, so we don't have much of a choice."

"Kierran?" Alannah squeezed his hand. "We can take you offworld to a human hospital. As soon as Richard and Eddie come back, we can do that."

Kierran met Alannah's glance. "No," he said. He wasn't going to ask how much higher the risk was or how much it would hurt afterward. All that was unimportant because even if they told him he was going to die, he knew he would prefer that to going back, though right now, he was hazy on the details of why.

"Okay. I'll be right here when you wake up," Alannah said.

"All right, doctor. Put him under," Jerra said, "so I can get to work."

The doctor tied an elastic band around Kierran's upper arm and stuck a needle into it. "Do androids dream of electric sheep?" she asked.

Kierran frowned. He opened his mouth to tell her he was not an android, but then the vision of his one functioning eye greyed out and a leaden blanket was pulled over him.

When Kierran next came to, it was to a world of pain. He fought to gain some semblance of control, instinctively lashed out, grabbed hold of something, or someone.

A yelp that wasn't his. Kierran was squeezing the doctor's wrist. She was holding an ICD unit. He let go. Realized he had used his inorganic right hand. Realized both of his eyes were working.

"Welcome back, and please don't try to kill the person who is doing her best to keep you alive," the doctor said, putting down the ICD unit on a table. She touched her wrist gingerly and grimaced.

"All systems are back online," said Jerra.

"Clearly," the doctor huffed. "I'm tempted to kill you again," she added to Kierran. "You could have broken my wrist."

He wanted to apologize, but he was distracted by insisting pain. "My pain suppressors," he gasped.

The doctor glanced over at Jerra.

"They should be—" Jerra cut themself off. "Whoa. Something is going on in the hippocampus and the amygdala."

"Something?" echoed the doctor.

"Neurotransmitters are all over the place," Jerra explained.

Kierran had no idea what that meant. All he knew was that it wasn't very pleasant.

"What's going on in your head right now?" the doctor asked.

He had lost his right arm in the accident. He had lost his left eye. He had lost more than that. He was alone, and he could not afford artificial parts, and he had indebted himself for life already to have that life saved, whether he had asked for it or not.

"Kierran?"

The vision of his one remaining eye blurred with tears.

"There is a new military program that you might be interested in."

He wanted to wipe his eye, but his right arm was not there anymore, and his left side was sporting too many IV ports and monitoring equipment to be of any use.

"What program?" he asked.

"What?" the doctor said. "Kierran, can you hear me? Jerra, what is happening?"

"I'm not sure. Look at this."

How many doctors were in the room?

"Does it mean I will be completely free of debt when it's over?" Kierran asked.

"Kierran, we're helping you free of charge," the doctor said. "Kierran?"

He blinked. He could see her clearly now. More clearly than his vision ever was, even before he lost his eye. "Why can I see?" he asked.

"Jerra replaced the damaged parts in your head," the doctor said.

"I'm not sure he can hear you," another voice said. Jerra's.

"I can hear you," Kierran said. Or thought he said. What he heard himself say was, "I need to think about it."

"Did you break his mind in the process?" The doctor again, frustrated.

"This has never happened before."

"Has this happened to you before?" That question directed at Kierran.

"Yes," he said. "Some of it."

"Okay." The doctor turned her back to him and walked out of the room.

"This is not my fault!" Jerra called after her.

Kierran lay staring at the ceiling. He logically knew he shouldn't make life-altering decisions in his current haze of pain meds and shock. They had offered him a talk with a psychologist, but he had declined for obvious reasons. It was units he didn't have. Even so, he already knew what he was going to decide. No amount of drugs could disguise that from him. There was only one option.

Voices again. Kierran tried to raise his head to see them, but ended up having to wait until the people who had entered came into his field of vision.

"What do you mean, cognitive abilities?" a woman's voice asked. It was comforting and familiar.

Kierran tried to smile when he saw her. She looked so worried that he had to do something to alleviate it, even if he was the cause of her concern. Even if he only wanted to cry again. "Hi," he said, his voice raw and breaking. "Mom."

"Oh sweetie, I'm not..." Not his mom. Someone else. How had he ever mistaken her for his mom? The two did not look remotely alike. And besides, his mom was—

"Is he hallucinating because of the drugs?" the woman with the kind face asked.

"Alannah," Kierran decided with finality.

"Yes," Alannah agreed.

"It's not the medication," the doctor said. "It would make him drowsy, yes, but not..."

Kierran blinked against the overlapping images his implants were firing at him, trying to sort out what went where.

"His brain is all but inactive," Jerra supplied. "This is... a lot."

"What happens after this?" Kierran asked, hoping he was asking the right person. It was like trying to have multiple chats open at the same time and give the right answer to the right person blindfolded. Blind... Maybe that was the key to determine which conversation he was talking into?

"After the contract terminates, you will be free of debt. You keep the prosthetics and the implants available to civilians."

"And I will be free, then?" One eye not there now.

"Kierran, who are you talking to?"

Kierran blinked. Perfect vision now. "Not you," he told Alannah.

"Wait," Jerra said. "I think I get it. It's not his cognitive abilities or hallucinations at all."

"Take your time, Jerra." The doctor. Not sincere.

Lack of vision in Kierran's left eye. "I just need to think for a little while," he said.

"It's memories."

"Come again?"

"Look." Jerra talking. "These are memories. He is reliving his past."

"Why? What did you mess up?" The doctor, the one in the present, annnoyed.

"I didn't mess anything up. I repaired him! He's not a cooler unit. It's not that simple."

Kierran wished he were a cooler. Coolers had one task and things must be extremely uncomplicated for coolers.

"Why? You said you could fix it."

"No," Jerra retorted. "You are missing the point. I *repaired* him. Here. Do you know how to read this?"

"Please, could someone explain it? Pretend you are talking to someone who doesn't know anything about neurosurgery or psychosurgery. Which you are." Alannah. Upset.

Kierran closed his eyes. He had such a headache and their bickering was only making it worse. And he did not want Alannah to be upset. He tried to tune out their voices.

"Kierran?" the doctor said.

Kierran opened his eyes again. Consulted his inner chronometer and found that it was working now. He had missed two minutes and seven seconds.

"You had your implants installed when you signed up for the enhanced soldier program, right?"

"Yes," he said. "And the prosthetics."

"Did you have anything removed when you... left?"

Kierran blinked. Again the vision in his left eye failed.

"We have great results with the procedure," the doctor explained.

"Will I have no memory of..." Kierran had to clear his throat. "Of anything before? Are you going to remove everything?"

"Nobody is removing anything, son," said the doctor. "It's an offer we extend to ease you into your new life. You are not trained to handle trauma, and dwelling on all this..." The doctor gestured to Kierran, meaning his missing eye and arm and barely healed bruises and cuts, or rather the cause thereof. "It can take focus away from your new life. There is no reason to bring all this with you. But it's up to you. It's a simple procedure, really, once we are working on you already. We just cut a few—"

"—neural pathways that were not active before. Kierran?"

"Memories," he said.

"Yes, exactly," the doctor agreed.

Alannah looked horrified. "Did you agree to that?" she asked.

"Yes," Kierran said.

"We will need you to sign the agreement, of course," the doctor said.

"Of course," Kierran agreed, wondering how. Wondering if he would be able to use his left hand. Wondering if an artificial arm would feel like a real arm. He blinked.

Alannah was back. "Oh," she was saying. "Kierran, do you want to..?"

"Before you go down that wormhole," Jerra said, "I would advise strongly against severing the connections again. At least anytime soon. I don't want to go back in now. It's too risky. And besides, I have some ethical qualms. One thing is doing repairs I'm not supposed to. Cutting off parts of the brain is completely different."

"Kierran! You need to breathe," the doctor was saying.

There was another blank of 34 seconds in his memory.

"Take a few deep breaths," the doctor said. "You need to leave now," she said, not to Kierran. "He needs rest."

Someone, Alannah from the feel of it, touched Kierran's shoulder briefly.

Kierran closed his eyes.

Once humanity discovered through trial and error that computers and artificial intelligence were not able to safely navigate what we call hyperspace (a term that, rightly so, indicates that it is more a place than a certain speed), the next logical step was to add a human pilot to the equation. Other species use pilots for the same purpose too. No matter how advanced, technology alone cannot perform sufficiently in the strange pocket of folded space that faster-than-light travel demands. Whether due to natural evolution, training, or special abilities an individual is born or hatches with, our fellow category 3 species all produce individuals who are suited for hyperspace piloting.

Although tests indicate that people of certain neurotypes adapt better to the conditions, no human has the innate abilities to perform adequately in hyperspace, however. It has been speculated that given what we know of the qualities needed for the task, the ability may be cultivated over time, but it is a long process, and we are not going to wait for evolution or purposeful breeding to provide a potential solution before undertaking interstellar travel.

The answer to our troubles is a substance simply known as hyper. This drug temporarily enhances an individual's reaction time and sharpens their senses to such a great extent that it enables them to easily and safely navigate hyperspace. With a short half-life and practically no side effects, hyper is the perfect solution to the faster-than-light problem.

If you are interested in an exciting career that will literally take you across the vastness of our galaxy, enable you to meet people of all species and ensure you have a job that never gets monotonous, Trans World Trading is the perfect place for you. We are currently offering free training for persons who qualify in the initial aptitude tests and sign a two-year contract with our company.

Anyone is welcome to apply, but for more information about suitable neurotypes and relevant abilities, such as hyperfocus and fast reaction time, please see the linked VoidPage.

— Outdated information from TransWorld Trading's VoidHub

13
EDDIE SHOWTIME

If there was one thing Eddie excelled at, apart from the obvious, it was compartmentalizing bad shit. So she packed away any concern for Kierran, for Raithan, and about the *talk* Richard was definitely going to have with her about hyper after this.

The obvious thing she scored full marks at was going extremely fast without wrecking anything, especially when she was hopped up on hyper. Usually speed meant faster-than-light travel. Today, it meant something that felt to Eddie like a modest pedestrian pace but which caused her passenger to clamp his teeth shut on terrified yelps and hold on to his seat although he was safely strapped in.

"Be careful!" Richard told her.

"It's a groundwheeler!" Eddie laughed, swerving around another groundwheeler and then back into the other lane to overtake yet another. The moment she leapt into the driver's seat, she had muted the groundwheeler's warning systems and overridden the protocols for safe driving with Chrys' ridiculous code. Apparently, this little thing could pack an impressive speed for such a vehicle when in emergency mode. "Do you realize how much faster a spaceship goes?

Do you realize that when I say 'course correction' in space, it means I'm keeping us from getting smashed to atoms on a stray asteroid in less time than it takes you to say 'badass'? This is easy!"

"I'm starting to see why no one ever thought hyper was a great idea for drivers of ground vehicles," Richard muttered. He was clearly trying to keep his cool.

"I don't. Even AI systems fail to pick up on a danger sometimes," Eddie said, possibly too fast for Richard to catch it. She glanced at the tracking signal hovering in the air projected by his patch. "He's stopped moving," she said.

Richard made a noncommittal sound. "I'll get hold of Raithan's emergency contact. Whatever that means," he added under his breath.

"My units are on a team of undercover agents working with him," Eddie mused.

"Since Chrys had the information for this kind of scenario, I hope so," Richard said, swiping another display into the air to make the call.

"Otherwise we'll take care of stuff." Because Eddie was all instincts and reactions and action, and she could do anything right now.

"If by 'stuff' you mean the two of us charging in without backup to neutralize a gang of heavily armed wendek and safely extricating Raithan at the same time, I would rather not—"

"Okay, shortcut!" Eddie called out and made a sharp turn across the road.

Richard, thinking it was one of those situations where she needed to concentrate and he had better keep quiet, didn't make a sound as Eddie turned, cutting a corner and narrowly avoiding clipping a parked groundwheeler.

"I'll make that call," Richard said when they were speeding straight ahead on the next street. Only a few turns before they headed out of Kwipadam.

Eddie only caught a quick glimpse of a wendek with dark green hair on Richard's display because however good she was, she did need to look at the road ahead.

"Hello?" the wendek said in Standard.

"This is Richard Hart of *Colibri* Investigations," Richard said. "We are investigating a case in Kwipadam with Raithan WeinZalneinth."

"Yes, I know. My name is Kellieth ReinAraneinth. I'm his assistant. How may I help you? Why are you calling me?" the wendek asked.

"Raithan is currently missing. We—"

"Is your patch secure?" Kellieth interrupted.

"Yes," Richard said, annoyed because he was a former intelligence officer and of course his patch was secure, and so on. "We need backup. Raithan was abducted by the arms dealers he was working on exposing. We have his exact location. Can you send your people to help?"

A person working at normal speed may not notice the delay in Kellieth's response, but Eddie winced. All delusions of an army of secret agents disappeared. Backup may only be something Raithan took of the files on his patch.

"It's... only me and Beth. And I'm not suitable for this kind of work."

Beth was a Synal name, unlike Raithan and Kellieth. It was also, Eddie mused while she was driving and trying to find a solution at the same time, a name that existed in English and probably a bunch of other human languages. In English, it was mostly used by people who identified as female, but for wendek, it could belong to any gender like all Menal and Synal names. And a different part of her brain had come up with a solution now. "I have an idea!" she shot in.

"No," Richard said.

"Just listen!" Eddie told him.

Both Richard and Kellieth did. It took a couple of seconds for them to get it. There was a faint noise of a siren approaching them from behind.

"That is not an idea! It's a complication!" Richard growled.

"No! Half of Kwipadam's traffic control corps is probably following us. They can be our backup!" Eddie laughed.

"But they are not—" Richard began.

"No, your driver is right," Kellieth said. "Raithan doesn't want to involve anyone who could complicate things, which means several of the criminal offense departments, but the traffic control corps will not be a problem. If you are fast enough—"

"Please," Eddie scoffed. She sped past a very obvious stop light, rounding another corner and sending the groundwheeler careening onto its three side wheels before it bounced back down.

"Yes," Richard said, trying to look like he didn't want to murder Eddie. "But they have no idea what they are walking into. These are armed criminals!"

"I know. But they are equipped to deal with drivers escaping a crime scene or who will do anything to avoid law enforcement for whatever reason. I'll notify them in time to prepare them, but not in sufficient time for anyone we don't want to make it to the location," Kellieth said.

"Right. About the backup you can provide..."

And then Eddie decided to zone out on the conversation. Not because she couldn't concentrate on driving, but because it was slow and getting tedious. All she needed was the basics.

By the time Chrys' nifty little groundwheeler approached the location, Eddie estimated that they were ahead of the traffic control corps by five minutes. Richard had talked to the person called Beth who would be there only a little bit after that, and Kellieth was notifying the squad following them.

Eddie was glad they had a precise tracking signal because this was not a small place to search for a person. It was a chick port that looked more private than commercial, by which she meant more shabby and unused than anything public on a wendek planet ever did.

Richard was out of the groundwheeler the moment Eddie stopped it. "Raithan should be somewhere in the back of that building," he told her. "Stay behind me. We can't know if they found his tracker and are waiting for us."

"Right," Eddie agreed. She knew she shouldn't feel disappointed that they didn't get to go in the front with guns blazing. That was the hyper talking. Richard was moving so damn slowly, though. Did he think he was less likely to be spotted by lack of speed alone? That made no sense.

"Eddie, tone down your impatience," Richard said. How could he even tell?

And Eddie, of course, had no way of replying that he would catch. "Sure, Dick," she muttered.

There was only one door nearby. Locked, of course. "Can you open it?" Richard asked.

Eddie studied it and turned back to him. "I need my tools. Or we can use brute force, but it might alert security."

"Is there anything here you can use?"

The ground was littered with scrap metal and plass, and Eddie began to look for something that could be turned into a lockpick when alarms started blaring from somewhere on the other side of the building.

"Brute force!" Richard decided.

Eddie whooped and took out the kinetic gun she had snatched in the hotel. Before Richard could order her to let him do it, she sent a volley of shots into the door around the lock. Some of them hit the lock itself too and became embedded in the metal, making it impossible to use normally ever again. But the effect was exactly what she had hoped for. One well-aimed boot heel, and the mechanism fell off, clattering to the floor inside the building. Another kick, and the door gave in.

Richard brushed past her. "Thank you, Eddie," he said in a strained sort of voice. "How much ammunition do you have left?"

"Erh... A bit, I think?" she replied as she followed. Okay, so maybe she had overdone it, but her aim was good, and it was fun to use a real kinetic gun. The recoil was completely different from dart guns.

"Don't shoot at anything else unless it's an absolute emergency or I give the order," Richard continued.

Eddie rolled her eyes.

They found themselves in a corridor that smelled faintly of biological garbage that hadn't landed in the right waste container for recycling. Which was weird in a wendek facility, but then, said facility was clearly in disrepair. Paint was peeling off the walls, and it looked like Wenamak's native wildlife had enjoyed picnics in the corners.

They passed an open door, and Eddie peeked into a mostly empty room with some dust-covered metal furniture stacked in one corner.

The corridor forked up ahead. Richard stopped and pointed to the right, then at Eddie. She nodded, and as Richard rounded the corner to the left, she went right, gun at the ready. The place was still empty and silent apart from faint shouting and gunshots in the distance.

They were clearly missing the main event. If this was fiction, what Eddie and Richard were actually doing would be relegated to some side characters and a subplot.

Odd how all this felt unreal, in a way. Like having a dream or playing an immersive game or even just watching a show. Eddie knew that even though her senses were sharp and fast, hyper also made her feel detached from reality, which was probably partly the point because hyperspace was kind of adjacent to reality, and normal rules did not apply there.

"This way," Richard said and continued to the left. They came upon another empty door frame, and Eddie followed Richard inside.

And yep, this was indeed where Raithan was located. Alive, but a bit more worse for wear than the last time Eddie saw him.

The wendek agent was lying on the floor in an awkward heap. His hands and feet were tied to a metal chair that had fallen over or, Eddie thought, that he had toppled over in an attempt to free himself. His otherwise perfect blue hair was a mess, and he had a split lower lip that had bled impressively on his previously white suit.

"Is that Beth fighting them?" was the first thing Raithan said.

"Yes," Richard answered. "Along with traffic control."

"Traffic control?" the wendek asked.

"I'll fill you in later. How badly injured are you?" Richard said.

Raithan scoffed, then winced. "I can walk, and I can shoot if you have a spare weapon," he said. "I assume you are here to remove me before anyone decides to use me as leverage?"

"That too," Richard said, neglecting to explain that Chrys had pretty much twisted their metaphorical arms. "I need a knife."

"Ah, allow me to provide…" A gasp of pain. "Sharp metal, over there," Raithan finished.

Eddie realized that as much as she sometimes enjoyed seeing posh and powerful people removed from the bridge of their fancy Laridae class ships, she liked Raithan too much to find this funny at all. "On it," she said, spotting the piece of jagged, rusty metal sticking out from a pile of pipes and rebar on the floor. "Were you trying to get that?" she asked, impressed.

"Yes," Raithan said.

Eddie was bending down to pick up the appropriate tool when running footsteps in the corridor rang out. A wendek appeared in the doorway and skidded to a halt when he discovered the prisoner wasn't alone anymore. Another one was right behind him, already aiming a weapon at Richard's back.

Eddie picked the nearest metal pipe off the ground and leapt forward, doing the kind of almost instant calculation she needed to do when flying through hyperspace as she moved. The projectile from the kinetic weapon hit the metal pipe, and the impact reverberated through Eddie's hands, making them numb and tingly. She charged at the first wendek and hit him with the pipe, and as he was going down, she batted away the second wendek's gun and then clubbed her with the pipe too.

She turned around, desperately trying to come up with something cool to say, but her mind really was a lot better at action than words in these types of situations, so all she came up with was, "Don't mess with Eddie Showtime."

Richard had turned around and was lowering his gun. His reaction time was laughable compared to Eddie's right now. He probably hadn't even noticed what was going on before Eddie intercepted the projectile. He made a sound that sounded like a mix between a growl and a sigh. "You'd better keep watch," he said with what must be an enormous effort. "Hand me the sharp piece."

Eddie did so.

"You gave my pilot hyper," Richard said to Raithan.

Eddie looked over her shoulder to see Raithan's mouth stretching in a smile, blood leaking from his split lip. "Yes," he said, "And I am not regretting it at all."

Eddie laughed and turned back to the door as Richard began to work on the ropes holding Raithan. No one else appeared in the doorway before he finished.

Behind Eddie, Raithan hissed in pain.

"Careful," Richard said.

Eddie briefly looked back again to see Richard helping Raithan to his feet. She knew wendek skintones well enough to tell that he was pale and looked sick, though.

"I should get to Beth," Raithan said.

"You aren't in any shape to help her," Richard told him. "They didn't go easy on you."

Raithan tried to scoff. "They didn't get far. And they were amateurs," he said. Eddie did not want to think about the implications of that statement. What kind of life did you have if you ranked torture skills?

"Regardless, you would only complicate things right now," Richard said.

"Then let's get back to Chrys' groundwheeler first. She keeps pain medication in it," Raithan said.

"How do you know we used hers?" Eddie asked.

"You must have gotten my location from her, and her groundwheeler accounts for your speedy arrival," Raithan said, impressively logical for someone in his situation.

"Yeah, and also because I'm a superb driver," Eddie said. "Thanks to you."

Richard mumbled something under his breath that Eddie didn't catch. Probably another complaint. "Take the lead, Eddie," he added.

Eddie happily did. They did not meet anyone on their way out, and it also sounded like the fighting on the other side of the building was over.

"Will you let them know we got him?" Richard asked as he helped Raithan into the groundwheeler.

"Sure," Eddie said and called Alannah. She was starting to come down from the hyper. She hated that part. It was like walking through a bog, or how she imagined that might feel. It was sluggishness and irritation, and exactly because she was coming off the high, she knew snapping at people wasn't a good idea.

Alannah was not taking the call.

Eddie tried calling Chrys instead.

Raithan and Richard were talking about the kidnappers throwing away Raithan's patch on the way here and his having a tracker in his shoe exactly in case something like that happened, and Eddie also did not want to think of how often the man had been abducted and whether he took all kinds of precautions all the time.

Eddie moved into Richard's line of sight. "Guys! No one is answering my calls."

"Maybe the surgery is taking longer than anticipated," Richard said.

"Surgery?" Raithan asked. "Was your friend from the fighting ring injured, Eddie?"

Eddie didn't realize Raithan had even seen Kierran there. "Yeah, he was shot," she told him, which was a gross simplification. "But even so, Chrys wasn't doing the surgery. Not Alannah either, obviously. We should get back there and check up on them." What if something had gone wrong and Kierran had snapped and attacked everybody? Fuck, why had they left Alannah and Chrys alone with him in the first place?

"Agreed," Richard said.

"I have to at least talk to Beth," Raithan said.

"You can use Eddie's patch to message her," Richard told him. "Eddie, get in the back."

"I can't drive from the backseat!" she protested.

"Get in the back," Richard repeated in a tone of voice that left no room for argument.

And since she was getting sober awfully fast and needed not to give him any more reasons to be cross, she complied.

Shortly after, as Eddie was handing over her patch to Raithan, a message from Alannah ticked in. "Everything is fine, we're just a bit busy. Hope you are all okay too." That was all. And it did nothing to alleviate Eddie's worry.

Mental health professionals had been treating trauma for centuries through therapy and medication when surgical procedures to remove the memories of a traumatic event became an option. That is not to say that surgery had not been *attempted* earlier in human history, but the ancient practices were extremely intrusive and had a very low success rate indeed. If you are historically inclined, you may have heard the term lobotomy, a type of brain surgery which attempted to pacify a patient by cutting the connection between the frontal cortex and the thalamus. Often, this procedure would render the patient incapable of normal functionality. Later, the procedure was replaced by cingulotomy, a more refined way to deactivate parts of the brain which caused patients great distress. This, however, was meant to be a last resort as the surgery was still quite drastic, especially by the standards of our day and age.

Modern psychosurgery is a lot less invasive and without most of the risks associated with what we now must think of as failed experiments of earlier times. In theory, what surgeons can do today sounds nearly perfect: Precise surgery that can cut off certain memories and the psychological responses connected to them.

If you are wondering why you have not heard of the practice (or, if you are struggling with trauma, been offered it instead of therapy and medication) in the light of how simple it appears to be, this is why: Despite the progress, it is still impossible to control the procedure sufficiently.

When finding a connection to sever in order to remove the memories of a particular traumatic event, the event itself often cannot be pinpointed precisely enough. For one thing, it can be a series of events and not one single catalyst. And even when it is only one event, the human brain is too complicated for us to separate healthy from unhealthy coping mechanisms, and in the case of older trauma, it has often become an ingrained part of the patient's understanding of their own self.

In this paper, we will attempt to determine whether psychosurgery will ever become a viable option for humanity. Can it, in other words, ever replace other methods of trauma treatment?

— Doctor Sheng Qiuyue, excerpt of *A Treatise on the Evolution of Human Psychosurgery*

14
THE MECHANICS OF MEMORIES

Kierran O'Connor assessed his situation.

He was fine.

He was fine except for the fact that his whole world had come tumbling down, and every time he tried to think of his past, a pit opened up somewhere inside him, and when he tried not to think of it, he felt even worse. He was fine except for the bit where he had just had brain surgery and his pain suppressors did not seem to be as efficient as before.

He was fine.

The wendek surgeon was gone. So were Richard and Eddie, and Kierran felt bad about that although he had not been in a state to notice their leaving and much less to help them. And why did he feel he ought to help them? To atone for everything he had done? Hah. That was a meager start.

He shifted in the bed. Between them, Chrys and Alannah had moved him into a room that Chrys kept for overnight patients. Although he had never been here before, he could guess why she had it. He had heard about her. The human doctor who would treat the less fortunate and accept that someone who fought in an illegal fighting ring for a living may not want to go to the hospital.

In a recent past, Kierran would have declined any help, medical as well as physical support. He wasn't too sure he could stand anyone's touch now, either, but for different reasons. And he had been too drugged and confused to even attempt to protest Chrys and Alannah's aid. Besides, this was a different life. Quite literally because apparently, he had been effectively dead for a minute.

Most of his memories had to do with the accident. With his military training. The things they had made him do to see if their modifications had worked. Had he been a soldier or a test subject? Both. It was not strange that the enhanced project had been a clandestine enterprise, nor that it had been forcefully shut down. Kierran tried to swim back further. To a happier time. One when his mother was alive. One when he was dreaming of the stars and studying, learning how to repair and maintain the ships that took people there...

"Kierran?" Alannah's voice.

Kierran forced his eyes open.

Alannah was sitting on a stool next to the bed. She looked at him with a kind and concerned smile on her face, and Kierran hated it because he deserved nothing of the sort. "Hi," she said. "How do you feel?"

How did he feel? In that past life of his, he could have said, "with great difficulty", except he wouldn't have discussed it at all. Now, he felt all too easily. Too much. But he couldn't tell Alannah that.

"I'm fine," he said. His go-to response. And it wasn't a complete lie because he was not currently in excruciating pain, and he wasn't in immediate mortal danger.

A long, deliberate breath. "Kierran," Alannah began, "you don't have to—" A crash and shouting from the waiting room cut her off. Alannah turned and Kierran sat up, his head spinning and buzzing as the room lurched around him.

Someone cried out. Someone else yelled in Synal, of which Kierran's understanding wasn't great, but his translator implant was working perfectly. Besides, he would recognize a lethal threat regardless of the language.

Something happened inside of him that he didn't know how to describe. The recently dead Kierran stirred, and he was both relieved to the point of tears and terrified beyond words to feel that part of himself again. But this was no time to indulge in emotions, that part told him. He needed to act.

"Hide," Kierran told Alannah.

"What is going on?" she asked. Her voice had gone up in pitch, and her heart rate was elevated.

"I don't know, but I have to find— out." Kierran stumbled as he stood up.

"Kierran, you—"

"Hide, and don't get in my way," he said, and it was the old Kierran speaking, and he knew it was a reasonable demand, but he still felt strangely bad about talking to Alannah like that. No time to dwell on it. Kierran looked around for a weapon, but of course there was nothing, and anyway, he was a weapon himself, wasn't he? That's why he had this right arm of his, wasn't it? So he opened the door to the waiting room.

Chaos. As expected.

There was a slight delay in his perception, a discrepancy he was not used to noticing, and he couldn't tell if his artificial eye had slowed down, of if his brain was sluggish. Regardless, he spent full seconds taking in the scene and forming a plan of action.

Chrys was standing with her arms spread out, yelling at the intruders in a tone that would have made Kierran shrink away. She reminded him of his— No. No memories right now. He had to focus on the present. The doctor expressed signs of stress, but her body language was far more angry than frightened.

There were only four intruders, all wendek, which made Kierran physically superior under normal circumstances. They were facing the doctor, all armed, but not all comfortable with their weapons. One of them had toppled over a decorative lamp which was probably the commotion earlier.

"Don't make me ask again," the person who seemed to be in charge said. Kierran recognized her, but did not recall her name. "Hand over the humans, and we'll leave you alone."

"They aren't here!" Chrys told her. She was speaking Synal as well.

"One of them is standing right there," said another of the intruders.

Chrys looked over her shoulder at Kierran, her eyes going wide. "Get back to bed!" she told him, and he almost did turn around and leave at the tone of her voice, which was ridiculous.

He stepped forward instead. "We're the only humans here," he said in Standard because he did not have the presence of mind or the time to wait for a translation of what he wanted to say and then read it out loud. "You should leave now if you value your health."

Two of the intruders laughed.

And then the front door was flung open, and a figure stumbled through. "Doctor! Doctor!" she screamed in Standard. "Please help me! Please help—" She collapsed dramatically on the floor. And that was enough. All the wendek had turned to her in surprise, and Kierran was already moving.

He went for the leader of the group, knocked aside her firearm and pushed her against the nearest hard surface, a wall. This was no time for finesse. He slammed the back of her head into it, and she fell to the floor without a sound.

Kierran picked up her gun. It was a kinetic weapon. Good, he needed to—

"Drop it!" shouted one of the wendek. He had Chrys in a chokehold and was resting the barrel of another gun against her head.

Kierran immediately dropped his weapon, despite the part of his brain that screamed at him that one casualty wasn't a big deal as long as he took out the enemies. Blinding pain flared up in his head, paralyzing him for a moment.

There was a loud crack, and when his vision cleared, Kierran saw Chrys struggling with the man who had threatened her. He was still holding the gun, but his shot had gone wide and hit the water dispenser instead.

The two other wendek were advancing on Kierran. Which meant that no one was looking at the human who had collapsed on the floor, and Alannah had already gotten back to her feet and picked up a chair. Kierran saw her swing it at the man holding Chrys. Good. He estimated that the two of them could easily deal with him on their own.

So Kierran was free to take care of the remaining two. One had a baton in his hand that Kierran recognized as a stun rod, a weapon akin to a shocker. The other was carrying a kinetic gun which they clearly had no idea how to use properly.

Kierran went for the latter first, easily getting hold of the wendek's hand and dislocating their elbow. Kierran did not like the popping sound, and he liked the scream that followed an instant later even less, which was strange because, dead Kierran said, this was what he did. This was what he was meant to do. He was an enhanced soldier, supposed to fight efficiently and ruthlessly. Sympathizing with his opponent's discomfort was useless and irrelevant at best and a liability at worst.

The stun rod whizzed past Kierran's face too close for comfort as he dodged. He had had more than enough of electric shocks for one day. Probably, the rod did not have the power of the EMP gun, but even the idea of having his biotech messed up once more...

He and the stun rod's owner straightened up at the same time. A quick glance over his shoulder told Kierran that Chrys and Alannah were fine although they had their hands full. Chrys was talking at her patch while Alannah was making creative use of Chrys' disarmed attacker's waist sash tying him up. Good.

Stun rod guy tried to smash his weapon into Kierran's face. Kierran evaded again and stepped in close to disarm him. But in that moment, his vision decided to white-out for a second. It was long enough for the wendek to twist and use the momentum to push Kierran up against the wall. A display screen cracked, but it was security plass and didn't shatter. The wendek thrust his fist into Kierran's face. It hurt. A lot. It was astounding that he was not only able to feel pain so acutely but so many variations of it. This was a different pain from the one inside his head, but a split eyebrow had never hurt this much. This, he felt sick to realize, was pain how everybody else felt it. How people felt it when he—

Thankfully, though, dead Kierran knew what do to, or maybe it was just his training kicking in and his body acting on its own. He elbowed the wendek hard in the jaw, followed up by pulling down the man's head and slamming his knee up to meet it, and that was it.

Kierran's own legs gave out. He was relieved, and he was exhausted, and adrenaline was pounding through his veins, and his head hurt so damn much, and he— He was crying. Sobbing like he hadn't done for years. Since he joined the military. He didn't even know he was still capable of feeling this miserable and relieved and sad and guilty and confused. But then, he hadn't been able to feel all this before. And he wanted it to stop. He wanted to not have to deal with all these stupid emotions. He wanted not to have to deal with the memories of the past years connecting with the feelings they ought to have been connected to already but weren't.

"Kierran!" Alannah on her knees in front of him. Scared. Hurt? Was she hurt?

"Are you okay?" he choked out.

"I'm fine," she said. "We're all right. The peace corps is on their way, too. Kierran, look at me!"

He tried. She was blurry, and his face felt wet and his throat raw.

"Are you hurt, Kierran? Chrys! We need you!" The last bit she shouted over her shoulder.

"I'm fine," Kierran managed. Some habits died hard. Still, a split eyebrow wasn't exactly going to kill him. And, well, although that hurt, it was the other pain that felt unbearable.

"Kierran!" Chrys this time. Studying him. "Where does it hurt?"

Kierran shook his head, which made everything worse. "Not injured. Head," he said.

"Well, that's what you get for being an action hero when you're recovering from brain surgery," Chrys told him. "Other people wouldn't be able to even walk about that quickly."

Kierran wanted to tell her he didn't have much of a choice, but suddenly, relief won the battle of emotions, and he choked out a laugh, and once he had started, he couldn't stop again.

"Is this normal?" Alannah asked.

"I don't think anything here is normal," said Chrys, dryly. "He's in shock. Help me get him up and back to bed. I need to do something about that eyebrow, and check that he didn't ruin any of Jerra's work. Besides, we'd better keep him out of sight when the burglary department's people gets here."

[Connection established. Raithan has entered the chat. Kellieth has accepted the chat request.]

Raithan: This is Raithan. Status when you have a moment.
Kellieth: Are you all right?
Kellieth: Whose patch are you using? Please verify your identity.
Raithan: Scarlet fathe. And we should change pass phrase after this. Please remind me.
Kellieth: Yes, sir. Are you all right?
Raithan: Yes. Thank you for getting Beth on the case. Have you heard from her?
Kellieth: No, not since she engaged the arms dealers. Where are you?
Raithan: On the way to Chrys.
Kellieth: Are you hurt?
Raithan: Not badly.

[Beth has accepted the chat request.]

Beth: Mission accomplished. Local peace corps is here and taking care of the rest.
Raithan: Good to hear it. Beth, in case you haven't found them yet, one of my human friends neutralized two of my abductors, but they are still alive. I will contact you both again as soon as I have some privacy.
Beth: Understood.
Beth: Kellieth, I'll give you a full report in the meantime.
Kellieth: Thank you, Beth.
Kellieth: And Raithan?
Raithan: Yes, Kellieth?

Kellieth: Please listen to Chrys this time.

[Raithan has left the chat.]

— Written chat between Raithan WeinZalneinth, Kellieth ReinAraneinth and Beth WennanKwenenth

15
NOT VERY BRIEF DEBRIEFINGS

Eddie was talking in the back of the groundwheeler, and Richard glanced down at his patch to see what she was complaining about now. "I'm telling you," she was saying, "something is up! What if Kierran has gone completely insane and—"

"Eddie," Richard interrupted her, "that is not helpful. We're almost there." But he agreed that something definitely must be wrong. Alannah had only sent a short message and nothing else. Not even asking how their mission had gone was simply not her style.

Richard brought the groundwheeler to a halt outside the clinic, and things looked normal, but... "Eddie, with me. Raithan, stay here."

Raithan made a snort that might have been an attempt at derisive laughter. "Definitely not."

"You're injured," Richard told him.

"All the more reason to go see a doctor," Raithan argued. "And besides, Chrys' painkillers do wonders. But I'll let you lead."

Richard decided to accept that. Raithan wasn't endangering them, and it was not his responsibility to chaperone the wendek agent at this point.

There were no snipers lurking around the corners on the rooftops. In fact, nothing outside the clinic looked out of the ordinary at all. Richard would have liked to kick open the door to avoid any nasty surprises, but as it was, he had to wait for its motion sensor to register him and slide open on its own.

With his gun clasped firmly in both hands, Richard entered, Eddie behind him ready to provide backup, and Raithan bringing up the rear. And everything that had not been amiss outside was definitely amiss in here. The waiting room was a mess. Furniture toppled over, a cracked screen, a splatter of blood up one wall. The water dispenser was leaking and forming a substantial puddle on the floor, and Alannah was crouched, trying to mop it up with a towel.

"Don't shoot!" she shouted, as if Richard was in the habit of firing first and asking questions later.

Eddie said something behind Richard, and it wasn't too hard to guess what.

"I'm okay!" Alannah said, getting up and leaving the soaked towel on the floor. She looked utterly disheveled. "We're all okay! Are you okay?"

"We're fine," Richard said, though fine was a bit of an overstatement when it came to Raithan. But well enough to be on his feet and armed, at least.

Eddie brushed past Richard and embraced Alannah.

"I'm wet!" Richard saw Alannah say before his pilot obscured the view of her face.

Eddie replied something that was probably, "I don't fucking care," or something along those lines.

"What happened?" Richard asked. "Where are Chrys and O'Connor?"

Chrys appeared in the doorway to the next room. "I'm here," she said. "Kierran's resting." She looked as rumpled as Alannah.

Raithan said something and rushed toward her.

Richard caught her saying, "Raithan, you're hurt!" before the wendek embraced her.

"All right, where's O'Connor? I need to hug someone too," Richard muttered, hoping no one heard the dry sarcasm before he continued in a louder tone, "People! What happened?"

Chrys disentangled herself from Raithan. "We can tell you while I take a look at Raithan. Come on. I'll let you hug Kierran if you are very careful."

Dammit, so she had heard that. Richard sighed, holstered his gun, and followed the four of them into the adjacent room.

It was a small space that put Richard in mind of a rudimentary hospital room. Kierran O'Connor was lying in a narrow bed. His back was propped up by a couple of pillows. He opened his eyes when the group entered and looked for one absurd moment as if he intended to stand up. Richard motioned for him to stay in, he had to admit, much the same way he would have gestured for a pet to.

In the background, Chrys was herding Raithan onto a stool. Eddie said something Richard didn't see. He was busy studying O'Connor. The young man was looking even paler than usual, and there was a thin strip of wound sealant across one eyebrow and a fresh bruise around it. But it could be worse. He was alive and did look better than the last time Richard saw him. "Good to see you awake," Richard said. "I owe you thanks for taking that hit for me."

O'Connor's expression changed. He opened his mouth, then closed it again and shook his head.

"And I've got a feeling I owe you thanks for more than that. What the hell happened here?" Richard looked around. This room did look intact, but it had been a mess outside.

"Yeah, seriously," Eddie said. "We can't even leave you guys alone for a few hours."

Richard moved to stand with his back against one of the walls where he would be able to see everybody because he had a feeling this was going to be one of those conversations where everyone had something to say. Well, except O'Connor, maybe. Only Chrys had her back to Richard, but she was still working on Raithan.

"Alannah?" Richard prompted.

"Right," she said, perking up because this was the sort of delivery she felt at home with. "After you left, Chrys' surgeon friend arrived. They repaired the augmentation, if you'll pardon my lack of specifics here, that the EMP knocked out in Kierran's brain. Only—" She stopped herself, her eyes darting to O'Connor. "Only, while he was recovering, the clinic was overrun by members of the arms dealer gang who apparently had figured out Raithan has a connection to Chrys and... Honestly, I don't know what goes through the minds of people like that. They meant to kill Chrys. But it turns out that Chrys is not a pushover, and that even while recovering from brain surgery, Kierran is extremely efficient."

She was leaving out something important. Something about the surgery. Richard tried to figure out what, but only came up with negatives. O'Connor's face did not reveal anything but discomfort. But, Richard realized, it was a kind of discomfort he had not seen there before. He needed to address that. But not yet.

"Where are the intruders now?" Richard asked.

"Chrys called the peace corps to take them away," Alannah said.

"But weren't we supposed to not tip off the criminal offense department?" Eddie exclaimed.

Chrys turned her face for a moment, and Richard caught the latter half of what she was saying. "— And apart from that, burglary and interspecies affairs are two different departments, so it was not an issue."

"Indeed. Now, I would like a confirmation—" Raithan spoke up, then took in a sharp breath.

Chrys said something to him.

"Not to worry. I've had worse," he said to her with a smile that looked very private. "Anyway, a confirmation of who told the gang."

"What?" Eddie asked.

Richard saw where the agent was going with this.

"The only people who know about my operation are my assistant and my associate, *Colibri* Investigations and Chrys," Raithan went on. "There is only one other person who could have suspected anything. So how did you know, and why did you warn the gang?" This last bit was directed at O'Connor.

O'Connor looked even more uncomfortable. "I did not know about your operation," he said to Raithan. He looked away, then at Richard with visible effort. "But I saw Eddie with him in a bar," He motioned toward Raithan. Using his inorganic hand, Richard noted. "I didn't know why she was in Kwipadam and if you were too. Whether it had something to do with me."

"If you had asked me instead of running away, that would have been sorted out pretty quickly, you freak," Eddie said.

Alannah touched her arm and mouthed, "no."

"Go on," Richard said to O'Connor.

"I asked one of the gang members if she could find out anything. I didn't realize... I'm sorry."

Kierran O'Connor had not apologized after trying to assassinate Richard. He had never shown any kind of regret in front of the crew. Something definitely had happened during or after that surgery.

"Hey," Eddie said with a shrug. "That was really stupid, but don't beat yourself up over it. Shit happens."

"All right," Raithan said, "Can I use your patch for a while in private, Chrys? I need to make a few calls."

"Are you going to accept a no and let Kellieth take care of things for you?" Chrys, now standing so Richard could see her face, asked.

"No," Raithan replied with a smile that reminded Richard eerily of Micah Dietrich. "And besides, one of the calls is to them."

Chrys threw up her hands. "Fine. As long as you're here, I can keep an eye on you, at least."

Raithan climbed to his feet. "I'm going to need a detailed report from you, Richard."

"Of course," Richard said. And he was going to need Raithan to explain why he had given Eddie hyper.

"All right. Chrys?" Raithan stood up, hiding a wince.

"I'm not handing over my patch to you," she said. "I'll go with you if no one else needs medical attention right now?"

"We're all good," Eddie told her.

"Good. Then I'll go spy on Raithan," Chrys said.

"I appreciate that," Richard told her. Debriefings had never been his favorite thing to do on either side of the table. Now, he found himself on both. He ran his fingers through his hair and inhaled deeply. "All right. What went wrong with the surgery?"

"I wouldn't say anything went wrong exactly," Alannah said. "But Kierran should probably explain it."

Richard looked at him with encouragement.

"I... remember... things," O'Connor said, slowly.

"That's good?" Eddie prompted.

"Things I did not remember before. When I was recruited, they cut some connections in here." He pointed at his own head. "And... some memories were gone. When Jerra repaired me, they repaired... too much. My memories are back. And I— I feel different."

"You kind of look like they're pretty bad memories?" Eddie said, the edge gone from her tone.

O'Connor nodded and looked away. Richard was surprised to see him trying to blink away tears.

The room was silent for a while.

O'Connor finally looked back up at Richard. "I'm sorry," he said.

"For what?" Richard asked.

"All of it," O'Connor breathed.

"It's okay, sweetie," Alannah said.

Richard caught Eddie's eye. His pilot shrugged. Richard agreed. He had not expected anything like this, either. He cleared his throat. "Alannah is right," he said. "I can imagine it's quite a shock to you. So you should probably focus on recovering right now."

"I heal the same as before. Chrys says I should stay here for the day, and tomorrow I..." O'Connor shrugged in a way that suggested to Richard he didn't even know what came after that part of the sentence.

"Do you have any friends you can stay with?" Alannah asked.

O'Connor looked blank.

"Friends," Eddie repeated, "You know, not fans."

"I'll be fine," O'Connor said, which was an evasion if Richard ever saw one.

But what was Richard supposed to do about it? He could only imagine what regaining a lot of previously buried memories all of a sudden would do to a human mind. And with how upset O'Connor looked, it probably was not only the memories themselves. What had he said? "I feel differently." Richard had no way of verifying it, but his gut feeling told him the stress had been on the second word. That the enhanced soldier experienced emotions differently now. Richard wanted to get hold of someone in charge of the enhanced soldier program and shake them long and hard and ask a lot of very pointy questions. "Perhaps you should get some help," he suggested. That was what people did in case of mental issues. There was nothing odd about that. In his previous career, Richard had been required to talk to a military psychologist a few times a year to ensure he was at his best.

Alannah bobbed her head up and down enthusiastically. "I'm sure everybody in this room has sought out professional help at some point in their life," she said.

"I haven't," Eddie said. "But, I mean, it's totally cool if you need it."

"On that note," Richard said, "I need to talk to you, Eddie."

"Yeah?" Eddie smiled in what she probably thought was a disarming way, but really, it only got Richard more up in arms.

"Do you want to do it here, or should we go somewhere else?" He could put it off until they were back on the *Colibri*, but he hated waiting. He wanted it out of the way before he had to sit next to her in a chick and watch her pilot.

"Um, I could use some fresh air," Eddie said.

They went outside the clinic. The local star would rise soon. The clouds had drifted off, and Richard thought he could see a faint orange glow above the rooftops. It was still too early for anyone to be out and about, though. Richard was very much looking forward to going to bed as well. He was exhausted. Eddie ought to be too, but even if the hyper had worn off, it always took her a while to feel basic needs.

"What the hell were you thinking?" Richard rounded on her. "Our agreement does not end because some smug wendek agent hands you a dose of hyper!"

"I know!" Eddie told him. "I wasn't going to take it, honestly!"

"But then you very clearly did!" Richard almost shouted.

"Just let me explain, okay?" And explain she did. But as far as explanations went, this one was not particularly good. It rather sounded like an excuse to indulge herself, if Richard was honest.

There was a good reason they had an agreement about hyper, and apart from the legal aspects from a spaceship owner's point of view, it was for Eddie's own good. Richard had seen what a hyper addiction could do to a person. "That is not good enough, Eddie!" he said.

"What the fuck should I have done? Gone along with Kierran's idea and been humiliated or, you know, beaten up?" Eddie asked.

"Yes," Richard said.

She opened her mouth, then closed it again without a word and began to unwrap her hands, not looking at him.

"Do you think I enjoy having to make sure you don't go down that path again?" Richard asked.

Eddie raised her head. "This is literally the first time I have taken any without your approval! And it's not even because I wanted to."

"Isn't it?" Richard asked, meeting her gaze, daring her to lie to his face. "Can you honestly say that you did not want to take that dose from the instant Raithan gave it to you?"

Eddie finished unwrapping her hands and stuffed the strips into a pocket. "No," she admitted. "I mean... That's what hyper does to you."

"Hence why I am the one controlling your access to it," Richard told her.

"I know!" Eddie said. She ran her fingers through her hair. "It's not like I'm going to spiral out of control because of this. Also, if I hadn't done it, things might have looked a lot worse for you. For all of us."

Richard did not rise to that bait. Yes, something good had come of it, but if he admitted that, she might be looking for other desperate situations to justify her abuse. There was another persistent source of unease vying for Richard's attention, but he would have to deal with that later. Because Eddie was right, and she was one of two people who had directly saved him from a possibly fatal shot during this whole mess, and that was simply not good enough. He would have to review his own performance, too, but his crew did not need to know anything about that.

"So, what are you going to do?" Eddie asked. "Fire me?"

Richard gave her a few long seconds to really consider that option. "No," he finally said. "But consider this your first and final warning."

Eddie bit her lip. She looked genuinely upset. Her expression told Richard everything he needed to know. "Understood," she said.

Richard hated this. He didn't even think it was entirely fair to be this hardline about it given the circumstances. But he knew what it meant to be a commanding officer, and he would rather upset her now than see her give in to temptation again and again. Nip it in the bud. "Good. No need to discuss it further, then," he told her. "Let's go back in."

"You go on ahead. I'll be there in a minute," Eddie said and turned away from him, putting a stop to any further conversation.

Dear Micah,

Thank you for your fascinating explanation of the history of manual writing on your species' planet of origin. As you undoubtedly know, we wendek pride ourselves almost as much in our long tradition of calligraphy as we do our history of dance, incense and perfumes. I was, however, not aware that writing by hand as a practical means was prevalent so far into a technologically advanced age in your culture, and I did not know it was possible to do so with such simple elegance. I shall be sure to bring that up in conversation whenever someone lumps in humans with draevere in polite wendek society.

As you can see, my calligraphy still leaves a lot to be desired compared to your excellent penmanship, but encouraged by your fervor, I have decided to practice and have acquired an antique brush and traditional nanthe reed paper for the purpose. I should very much like to sample one of your culture's fountain pens if the opportunity arises.

You also have my gratitude for your recommendation regarding the hired help I inquired into. You can imagine my surprise when I learned that a dear human friend of mine is an acquaintance of a worker you have also employed. There are indeed wormholes everywhere as soon as you go looking for them, as they say. I quite agree there is no need to mention our chat regarding that coincidence to anyone, but I was very happy indeed with the janitorial services provided. Everything was cleaned up nicely.

Your devoted friend,
Raithan

16
Stray Cyborgs

"Yes, Alannah?" Richard said. He was sitting in the galley with his back to her. A patch display full of text was floating midair in front of him. Of course he knew it was her. Everybody's footfalls were different, and for Richard Hart, it was imperative to be able to discern these things when he couldn't just hear what she was saying.

Alannah had deliberately waited for the best time to approach her boss. Normally, she didn't tiptoe around anything, but this was a topic that required the right timing, and she could afford to wait for an opportunity because the *Colibri* was still docked at Wenamak's local space station. The delayed departure was officially caused by Richard needing to make a report to Raithan and have a conversation with him about offering hyper to spaceship pilots. Unofficially, Richard was deliberately denying Eddie the drug for a few days. Alannah had told Eddie it was okay to slip up once and reassured her that something really good had come of it because apparently, Alannah and Richard now had an unspoken good-cop/bad-cop agreement about this sort of thing.

Perhaps there was a third reason for the delay, as well. Alannah hoped there was because it would make this conversation a lot easier if Kierran was already on Richard's mind. She stepped around to the other side of the table. "May I?" she asked.

Richard made one gesture to swipe away the display and another to indicate the chair. "Go ahead," he said. He was looking a bit weary.

"I brought these back from Kwipadam," Alannah said and pulled up a genao model paste figure from her bag. She placed it on the table in front of Richard. "Space Crafts & Arts cured them for us."

"Why did you bring them with you?" Richard asked, shooting a disapproving glance at the snowman he had sculpted a few days back.

"Because we made them. They are part of our adventure on Wenamak," she insisted. "They will remind me of Raithan and Chrys and everything."

Richard held up his hands. "You can have mine. Dispose of it however you want."

"I will not dispose of anything!" Alannah told him. "But I will accept your gift and keep it with me." She patted the top of the snowman's head affectionately, then looked up at Richard. She should get on with what she was really here for. "How are you doing? You look tense."

Richard ran his hand over the stubble on his jaw. "I'm a bit tired of this job," he said. "Raithan is happy with how things turned out. He got the evidence he needed, and he says he was right to suspect that someone in the local interspecies affairs department was in on the gang's business, but I'm on a need to know basis."

Alannah could definitely see how that would frustrate anyone and especially someone like Richard. "That makes sense. There's probably a lot Raithan hasn't told us. But we did what he hired us to do, right?"

"Yes. But," Richard added, "this isn't what you're here to talk about, is it? Is Eddie complaining about me?"

"No, she isn't," Alannah said. "I visited Kierran."

Richard's expression hardened. "Yes?"

"He's not doing well."

"Chrys did what she could, but brain surgery isn't something you bounce back from. Even for someone like him."

Alannah shook her head. "That's not what I meant. You know that. Of course he is in physical recovery right now. But I'm talking about his mental state."

Richard inclined his head in agreement. "It will take a while for him to adjust."

"Adjust," Alannah said with a scoff that sounded more like the sort of noise that would come out of Eddie than her. "Richard, Kierran is traumatized. He has raging PTSD!"

Richard met her eyes. He leaned back in his chair and folded his arms over his chest. "Probably, yes," he said. "I'm not a mental health care professional. And neither are you, as far as I know."

"No, but I am human. I don't have to be a professional anything to see when another person is suffering!" Alannah exclaimed.

Richard winced. "I know. And your empathy is admirable. But my point is that what Kierran O'Connor needs is professional help."

"Is that it, then? He saved your life, and you are going to abandon him?"

"Alannah," Richard cut her off, "I did what I could. I made sure Chrys' got her associate to treat him, and you were there when I suggested he get help. What more do you want from me? I can't save everybody from themself."

"You saved me," Alannah said.

"That was a completely different situation. I'm not denying I wanted to help you, but I offered you a job because I thought you could be a valuable addition to the team."

"You saved Eddie," she persisted.

"Again, a completely different situation. She helped me solve a case, and I needed a pilot." He made a half-hearted shrug.

Alannah placed her hand on the table between them with emphasis. "But Kierran—"

"Alannah," Richard said, "what exactly is it you want me to do? Because if you have some insight that I don't, I would very much like you to share it."

"Offer him a job," she said, which wasn't exactly what she'd come to ask of him, but it was close enough.

"Offer him a job?" Richard echoed, clearly not convinced.

"Yes," Alannah insisted. "When we leave this system, take him along. It doesn't have to be forever. Just for a little while."

"And what then? Do you think any of us can give him what he needs? Wouldn't it be a lot better to find some contact info on a good mental health care provider and give that to him?" Richard asked.

"I mentioned that possibility to him again." Alannah clenched her fists to stop herself from fidgeting. "I don't think he's ready for it yet. I don't think he knows what he needs. But I am pretty sure he needs friends and a safe place to be. We can't just abandon him."

Richard made a face. He was reluctant, but Alannah felt she was getting through to him. "Suppose we brought him along. What would he do?" he asked.

"Well, he told me he was training to become a spaceship mechanic before he became a soldier," she said.

"But he was only in training. And he had no recollection of it until a couple of days ago," Richard argued.

"Still, he remembers now. Wouldn't it be handy to have someone on board who can do maintenance and minor repairs? Eddie knows a lot about ships, but when it comes to repairs, she's at the 'have you tried turning it off and back on' level, and the two of us are not even there," Alannah argued. "In addition to that, he has a unique skill set, and you know it. He could be an invaluable backup on missions."

"But as you said, he is not well. Do you think that arming him and taking him into potentially dangerous situations would be a good idea? And I don't mean for his sake only. I need to be able to trust my people," Richard said.

"And I get that," Alannah replied, "and I can't tell you whether he'd be okay right now for that sort of work. I'm not asking you to risk yourself or Eddie. In fact, please don't do that. But the *Colibri* has plenty of room for one more person, and again, it's not forever. I just... I can't stand the thought of leaving him behind right now."

Richard sighed. "Did you already talk to O'Connor about this?" he asked.

"No," Alannah said. "That's your turf, not mine."

"Are you sure?" he muttered. "Because it feels an awful lot like you're on my turf right now, then."

"I'm sorry, but this is what I do," Alannah said.

"Harass your employer to take on board stray, illegal cyborgs?"

"No, I *care*," Alannah said, and then, "but I suppose as a result, that's what I do too."

"Tell you what," Richard said with sudden briskness, "You convince Eddie this is a good idea, and I'll agree. And you get to make the offer to O'Connor, too."

"Deal," Alannah said.

"I'm sorry, what?" Eddie asked when Alannah broached the subject to her. She was awkwardly holding the vase Alannah had handed her a few seconds ago. "Look, I get that you want to help him out, but this is the guy who tried to kill Richard when we first met him, remember?"

"I know," Alannah said, "but at the same time, it's not."

Eddie looked confused. "Okay?"

"I mean, yes, it's him, but the military locked up so many of his memories. They changed him. And now that he has those memories again, he's changed back. I don't think he would ever become a hired killer again. That's part of why he's in such a bad state right now."

"Because he regrets killing random people for units?" Eddie said. "I get that, but he still did it."

"I'm not denying that. And neither is he." Alannah cocked her head. "Eddie, imagine we leave dock tomorrow and leave Kierran behind. He has no one. He can't even go back to the fighting ring because Raithan shut it down. And he is technically illegal, which makes everything more complicated."

"But we aren't his friends. Well, maybe you are, but Richard and I are not. And besides," Eddie said, "why can't he go back to the TDF and ask to have his enhancements removed?"

"Because he ran away in the first place and did a lot of illegal and horrible things. They wouldn't let him walk away."

"Do you seriously think Richard will let him on board?"

"Yes," Alannah said. She tried for a smile. Things had been tense between Eddie and Richard when they got back to the *Colibri*, but they were both trying to put the hyper incident behind them. "He will if you agree to it."

"Whoa, hold on!" Eddie held up both hands in front of her. "Richard said yes to this?"

"Only if you agree."

"Oh, nice," Eddie scoffed. "So he's making me the bad guy. That's such a dick move."

Alannah wasn't entirely sure this was the right time to laugh because important things were at stake here. "I don't think that's what he's trying to do," she said.

"Okay. Then what is he trying to do?" Eddie asked.

"Well," Alannah faltered. Began again, "Richard knows you weren't exactly thrilled to work with Kierran when we met him the first time. And while that was a thing Richard decided despite your feelings, it was in order to find out who wanted him dead. Those were special circumstances. This is different."

"These are not special circumstances?" Eddie asked.

"Well, yes. But different special circumstances. This is something we can do to help Kierran after he helped us out. That shot would have been lethal to Richard. Kierran saved him. But more importantly, it's about trying to help another human being. To help them get on a better path."

Eddie sighed. "Right."

"So my point is that Richard lets this be your call because he respects your opinion. He needs us all to cooperate and agree." At least, that was what Alannah hoped it was. Maybe even a consolatory move after dressing Eddie down about the hyper.

"Funny, he usually calls the shots around here," Eddie huffed. She ran a hand through her hair and then regarded Alannah seriously. "And you?"

"And me?" Alannah repeated. "What about me?"

"This was your idea, right? If I say no and we leave your little soldier boy behind, how are you going to react? I mean, I thought Richard was shrewd because he let me be the bad guy, but really it's worse. He is letting me be the bad guy in your eyes."

"Kierran is not my little soldier boy," Alannah objected, although that was besides the point. "Look, I know this isn't my call. Do I think we should bring him along? Yes. I do. For a little while, at least."

"And how long is that?"

"I don't know. A week. A month." Which was not at all enough for anyone to recover from what Kierran was facing. But it was a start. "With his physical recovery rate, he can probably help out with normal tasks. And didn't you once say it would be handy to have someone around with mechanical knowledge? Kierran happens to have that," she added.

Eddie's eyes narrowed. "And if I say no?"

"I'm not going to jump ship," Alannah said, which was probably what Eddie was considering. "I'm not going to make you an ultimatum if that's what you think. I'm only telling you how I feel. For all we know, Kierran might even decline."

Eddie groaned. "You're giving me that look."

"What look?" Alannah hadn't known there was a particular look she was giving anyone.

"The one that makes me feel like a terrible human being if I say no," Eddie said. "Okay, fine."

"Fine?"

"Ask him. I don't want to be the bad guy. Give him a couple of weeks to get back on his feet. Mental feet. Whatever."

"Are you sure?" Alannah couldn't help asking. "I don't want to..." What? Trade Eddie for Kierran? "I want this," she said, gesturing to the empty space between them. "I don't want to ruin our friendship."

Eddie looked surprisingly flustered for a moment, then recovered. "It's fine," she said. "I mean, I've been fucked up too. I didn't kill anyone, unlike soldier boy, but I get it. It's not going to ruin anything."

"Thank you," Alannah said. She closed the distance between them and pulled Eddie into a hug. "You and Richard act all tough, but you're good people," she added, squeezing Eddie and feeling her heartbeat against her ear.

"S—Sure," Eddie said.

Alannah stepped back and smiled at her. "I'll get things set in motion."

"One more thing," Eddie said and held out the vase with a pleading look. "Throw this out or something? I don't need a reminder of how bad I am at sculpting."

Alannah grinned. "All right. I'll take it. Richard didn't want his either."

"His was even worse than mine," Eddie said.

"I'll keep them."

"What? Alannah, no, they are ugly as fuck!" Eddie cried.

Alannah backed away from her. "Sorry, you gave it to me. It's mine now."

Eddie made a frustrated sound and shook her head. "Whatever. Just don't show it to anyone."

In this text, I have attempted to illuminate elements of wendek cultures and societies that you may not previously have encountered in entertainment or during brief visits to wendek planets and stations.

You may feel that parts of my essay seem like I am attempting to expose some kind of dark secrets that the wendek would prefer to keep safely behind pelso plating, but nothing could be further from the truth. This was never meant to be wendek-bashing.

I love a cup of freshly made twa. I enjoy genao model paste sculpting. I look forward to the next season of *Worra & Darith*. I also grew up on Tewamak where my family was part of a multi-species research group, and as such, I speak Synal as well as Standard and English. I lived in a wendek society practically all my childhood and teenage years. I have livelong wendek friends, and I have worked professionally with wendek as an adult.

I have, in other words, seen that wendek are far more than their entertainment and art. I have experienced the beauties of the species that we are all familiar with, but also the deeper layers of their rich cultures. Perfection is subjective, but still, no species is without flaws. There are speciest wendek, there is crime, and injustices happen in wendek societies like in any other.

I set out to write this honest account because glamorizing a species based on a glance at its surface is problematic, and it is also very close to objectification.

This is not to say that you can't enjoy what a species shows you via its entertainment and holiday resorts. I only question those who attempt to generalize based on what they see without going any deeper. Really, this goes for any species. Once you start looking, everything won't be how it first appeared. All species and societies have ugly sides and facets that they may not even fully understand themselves. And all that combined makes up a nuanced whole.

- And when you think about it, this isn't so different from individuals, is it? Only when you dive beneath the surface can you fully appreciate and understand someone, whether as a species or a person. Yes, it takes an effort, and both people and species are extremely complex. But if you put in that extra light year, you will learn and, in doing so, grow as a person yourself.

Do I know everything there is to know about wendek? No, I would never claim that. Neither do I know everything about humans - or even the people I share a living space with. We are all constantly learning new things about each other, and ourselves. And I think there is beauty in that journey.

— Alannah Jackson, postscript to *Why Wendek Are Not Space Elves*

17
FIRST STEPS

Every time he tried to make a decision or think about his current predicament, Kierran's mind snapped back like a rubber band and sent him reeling into his own past. It was incomprehensible how until a few days ago, what led to his joining the enhanced program was a blank. No, not even a blank. It had felt natural. Like nothing was missing. And now, there was so much more there, and he couldn't understand how he had never looked for it before.

Right now, he was struggling to stand up. It was not because of his physical health. Chrys had reassured him that despite his... what had she called it? Despite his 'being an action hero', he was healing inhumanly rapidly. Kierran did not feel heroic at all. He did feel inhuman, though. With all he had done while— He clenched his fists. Closed his eyes. He was here, *now*. But he was also *then*, in a past that refused to stay silent any longer and forced him to relive events as if they were happening to him right now.

With part of his mind stuck in memories he couldn't change, bringing himself to do anything felt impossible. At the moment, he was sitting on the edge of his bed. He was dressed, and his biotech rather than his stomach told him he should get something to eat. But his mind was woolly and strange, and getting to his feet was a huge task. All he wanted was to curl up and sleep, but even sleep was not as peaceful as it used to be.

The door chimed.

Kierran's body responded as if someone had forcefully intruded on him. He stood, ready to fight, before he even knew he had jumped off his bed.

He made his way to the door. It felt like a much longer journey than the five steps it took in his small apartment. The screen was showing a familiar face, looking determined and a little anxious. Perhaps if there was a dire crisis and he was needed to do something, to act rather than think, the past would leave him alone for a while.

Kierran touched the panel next to the door, and it opened. He almost closed it again because her presence felt so big. Not just because of what his biotech told him, but because he realized her determination and anxiety were for *him*.

"Hi," Alannah said. "I'm sorry for barging in. Again. Did I startle you?"

"No," Kierran lied.

Alannah smiled at him. "How are you feeling?"

"Fine," he continued to lie, and if he were the zetoi from that children's story, he would be dropping another feather. At his current rate, he would have very few feathers left.

"No, you are not," Alannah said, but she said it in such a quiet and kind way that Kierran didn't get annoyed with her. He got sad instead, which was worse. "How could you be?" she continued. "I can't even begin to imagine how confused and upset you must be."

Kierran shrugged, inadequately.

"If you want to talk about it... Your memories, or how you feel about them, then I want to listen."

She had said that before, and Kierran did not want to talk. And besides, he had no idea how to even start.

Alannah nodded as if coming to a conclusion, but it was such a tiny movement that only his augments picked up on it. They also told him she was experiencing stronger emotions than she let on. That, at least, he could relate to.

"I came to check up on you and talk about the future," Alannah said. "About where you go from here."

"I can still fight. Not here, I know. But somewhere else," Kierran said, though that tasted like a lie too. Sure, he could fight once he physically recovered. But he had lost something essential inside of himself. He had lost that cool, detached place, and he didn't think it was going to come back except in unpleasant bursts and fits as that dead part of him had done when Chrys and Alannah were in danger.

"I don't think that's a good idea right now," Alannah said.

No, it wasn't. But he hadn't asked her opinion. He looked away because her kind face made it impossible for him to say something like that.

"I have a suggestion," Alannah said. "Kierran, I think you should come with us."

Despite himself, Kierran looked back at her. She didn't appear to be joking. "What?" he said.

"I think you should come with me back to the *Colibri*. Come with us when we leave dock."

"Why?" Kierran asked. Alannah had shown him clips of cute animals the first time they met. It was not entirely unbelievable that she had thought of this idea and decided it was a good solution, but Richard and Eddie could not possibly agree.

"You haven't spent that much time with us," Alannah said, "but we all have our issues."

Kierran blinked. That was not where he had expected her to go.

"I grew up as a human child in a mostly wendek community," Alannah said. "I logically knew nothing was wrong with me or my family. We were just human. But I felt clumsy and weird. In one school I went to, I was the only non-wendek in my class, and the other kids would use scents I couldn't even pick up to communicate, and it made me incredibly insecure. I know this is a tiny thing compared to all that you have been through. I'm not telling you to compare our hurt. I only want you to know I get it."

Kierran did not reply. He was still not entirely certain where this was going or what he was expected to do with the information, but he couldn't bring himself to interrupt her.

"Eddie..." Alannah continued with a sigh. "Well, she was fired from the TWT because of her hyper addiction. She lost everything and was even homeless for a period of time. She is doing well now. But I can tell when it's been a while since her last dose that she's struggling with physical as well as mental withdrawal symptoms, and, well, you saw how easily she jumps at the opportunity when it is there."

Kierran made a small affirmative gesture. That he had definitely noticed.

Alannah went on, "Richard doesn't talk much about it, but he fell ill and found himself unable to understand what anyone was saying all of a sudden. And as if that shock was not enough, he lost his career path, and he had to learn new ways to communicate. He is pretty resolved about it. But I still sometimes see this look of anger and frustration on his face when he is excluded from a conversation because he can't see what people are saying. And the worst part is that it's not directed at them. It's directed at himself."

This was a strange re-take of their first ever conversation when Alannah had decided to defy the others and chat with him while they were on a job. But this time, the conversation wasn't about the team's hobbies. It was about their problems, and Kierran... Kierran was not certain he was even the same person as the one she had talked to then.

"Please believe me when I say I'm not telling you all this to compare your problems to any of ours," Alannah continued. "I'm also not saying you will magically feel better if you come with us. I'm only saying that we all get how sometimes you need a break. How you can need time to get things sorted out in your own head."

"I doubt the others would want me on board," Kierran said.

"Oh, they do. I've talked to them already," Alannah stated.

Kierran felt two things. He felt utter confusion because why would anyone want him near them? And he felt his throat seize up as he struggled to keep a sob down. "But— what would I even do?" he asked.

"You can help out with ship maintenance if something comes up. Give the *Colibri* a once-over. Save Richard a mechanic bill or two," Alannah explained. "Or you can help out with everyday stuff. Tidying up the galley. This isn't forever. Just come with us for a couple of weeks. Give yourself a breather."

Kierran looked away. He didn't want their charity. He didn't want anyone's charity. He didn't want to be a burden. He didn't—

"Kierran." Alannah touched his arm. She was smiling at him. "It's fine. It's okay to say yes. If you absolutely need a reason then you saved Richard's life putting yourself into harm's way. You can think of this as payback."

"But he already paid me back by getting me to the doctor," Kierran countered.

"Kierran," Alannah said again. "It's not only about units and favors. You can't put a price on someone's life."

There was no malice in her expression, but Kierran almost couldn't breathe. Because yes, you could. And thinking about it made him want to throw up.

"I'm sorry," Alannah said, seeing his ill-concealed discomfort. "But that? That is exactly why you should come with us. If nothing else, don't make me worry about you." And he must have looked as shocked as he felt because she continued, "Oh, come on. Of course I would worry about you, Kierran! Please give it a chance? I want you to come. I want you on the *Colibri*. And if you can't stand us, you can get off at our next stop."

Kierran tried to take a deep breath, but it hitched in his throat. He couldn't. He couldn't.

"Excuse me. I need water," he said and fled to the kitchenette. If he meant to use getting something to drink as an excuse, he ought to offer her something as well. But she stayed where she was while he stood bent over the kitchen sink, letting the water run to conceal the sound of his ragged breathing. He couldn't go with them. It was impossible. Even if Alannah meant what she said and, according to his implants, nothing indicated that she didn't, he still could not. Could he?

A memory forced itself into his head, one he had not been able to access for so long. This was not dead Kierran's memory. It was from before any of that happened. His mother, standing in another kitchen, handing an upset and much younger Kierran a glass of water. "When someone offers you kindness, you should thank them and take it," she said.

"You don't understand," he whispered to the memory. "After all I've done..."

Another memory. His teacher and mentor wiping his hands on a dirty rag after inspecting the inside of an engine. "Listen," the man said, "when someone offers you a good deal, you take it."

Kierran thrust his hands into the spray of water and ran them over his face. It was hard to argue with two people who meant so much to him, especially when they were long gone. He drew in a long, deep breath. Thinking logically about Alannah's offer, it was not a bad idea. They all knew what he was. Knew the risk they were taking by harboring a former enhanced soldier. And Alannah clearly was not lying. She really, truly wanted him to agree. He turned off the water.

Alannah was still standing there when he returned, waiting patiently for him.

Kierran swallowed. "Okay. Thank you."

"You will come with us?" she asked, sounding as hopeful as if he was the one doing her a favor.

"Yes," he said.

Alannah smiled. "I'm so glad to hear that. Can I hug you?"

"I don't know," he said, honestly.

"I'll try," Alannah told him. She put her arms around him and leaned her head against his chest. Held him tight for a moment. Then she stepped back. "Was that okay?" she asked.

"I— Yes, I think so," Kierran said.

She smiled again. "All right. Let's go pack up what you want to bring." She held out her hand.

It took a moment for Kierran to understand. Then he took it, tentatively, and it made her smile even more. And he had this strange and sudden feeling that although he was one big mess and nothing felt like it would ever be okay, he very much wanted to make Alannah smile, and that was something, at least.

ACKNOWLEDGEMENTS

You have reached the literary equivalent of a movie's end credits. Here, I get to thank all the awesome people who made this book a reality.

First, my thanks to Spaceboy Books for believing in my stories and offering me a cabin on their amazing spaceship. How cool is it that I get to roam the galaxy with *Colibri* Investigations and share their adventures? Thank you to Nate Ragolia especially for doing his editorial magic and being much better at coming up with snazzy back cover descriptions than I am.

My gratitude also to my wonderfully supportive family and friends who always have my back, and give me a space to rant about all the people living in the future/my mind.

Very special thanks to my team of beta and sensitivity readers Ashley, Christie Wilson, Gabe Clark, Hanna, Larna Holmes, Malene Marley Neergaard Momme, @naomisnovelnest, Philippe Moret, Sam Buchanan, Thomas Nielsen and Tiara Lockhart for providing me with invaluable feedback, asking all the right questions, and loving the *Colibri* family.

Also thank you to my Patreon supporters Gabe Clark, Ryan Watt, Skjalm, ZombiEdward and more. You rock!

Naturally, no acknowledgments are complete without my love to my feline trio, Reid, Dandy and Oscar, who keep me company and purr everything better (and occasionally nap on my keyboard or block my view of the screen, which is all part of their charm).

And thank you! I hope you've enjoyed this *Colibri* Investigations novella, and that you will join me for the next adventure.

The Terran Defense Force was more than an archaic military power flexing its muscles to discourage other species from getting any ideas. As it were, the number of open conflicts between the various Union species was minuscule. Officially, each species had a vast network of diplomats and embassies and negotiators. And then there was the less official side of things. The Force had deep cover agents stationed on every world. People going about their daily lives in whatever position they were put in and reporting back to a commanding intelligence officer.

Colonel Micah Dietrich was such an officer, and right now, they were watching a news feed in their office on Stonehenge Station. A wendek reporter was talking about the situation on a draever planet called Edaalen.

There was a genuine paper letter on Micah's desk written by one of their agents. Some correspondences were simply too delicate to risk leaving digital footprints all over the galaxy. The agent had recently, and correctly, speculated that something would happen to destabilize the political balance on Edaalen.

Micah took out a fresh sheet of paper from their desk drawer, submerged their fountain pen's nib in a bottle and drew up ink into the pen's reservoir. It was about time to give the agent some very specific instructions because Micah needed him to provide as much information as possible, but they also wanted him not to get into trouble.

ABOUT THE AUTHOR

Marie Howalt grew up near Copenhagen in Denmark, Scandinavia and decided to become a writer at the age of 11 when the local library failed to deliver an acceptable amount of science fiction and fantasy.

Having graduated with a master's degree in religion and English studies with a primary focus on speculative literature, Marie wrote as a hobby and worked as a teacher and a translator between English and Danish before changing lanes in life due to chronic illness (post concussion syndrome).

Nowadays, Marie writes as much as physically possible. The stories are hopeful and diverse and take place in the far future or other worlds.

When not writing (or bribing imaginary people to share their stories), Marie is dedicated to being a cat servant, but also enjoys reading/listening to audiobooks as well as drawing and collecting and restoring antique fountain pens. You can also find Marie pushing art supplies, stationary and fancy pens part-time in one of Copenhagen's oldest shops.

Marie's debut novel from Spaceboy Books, *We Lost the Sky*, came out in 2019. Since then, there has been a steady flow of a new book each year (plus the odd short story). What you have in your hands right now is the third novella about *Colibri* Investigations, and more stories about the little spaceship and its crew are on their way, along with a standalone spinoff set in the same universe.

If you want to keep up with Marie's life and writing (and cats! Cats are important), @mhowalt on Instagram is the indisputably best place to go. You can also get special perks and previews by newsletter or on Patreon via www.mhowalt.dk

ABOUT THE PUBLISHING TEAM

Nate Ragolia is a lifelong lover of science fiction and its power to imagine worlds more hopeful and inclusive than the real one. His first book, *There You Feel Free*, was published by 1888's Black Hill Press in 2015. Spaceboy Books reissued it in 2021. He's also the author of *The Retroactivist* (2017). His most recent book, *One Person Can't Make a Difference* (2022), was featured on Tor.com's Can't Miss Indie Press Speculative Fiction list, and was translated into Italian for Ringworld Sci-Fi in 2023. He founded and edited *BONED*, a literary magazine, and also created two webcomics. Nate is also a husband and a dog dad.

Shaunn Grulkowski has been compared to Warren Ellis and Phillip K. Dick and was once described as what a baby conceived by Kurt Vonnegut and Margaret Atwood would turn out to be. He's at least the fifth best Slavic-Latino-American sci-fi writer in the Baltimore metro area. He's the author *Retcontinuum*, and the editor of *A Stalled Ox* and *The Goldfish* for 1888/Black Hill Press.